FoR

BEST WISHES

www.Lee-McGeorge.co.uk

Cover Artwork: Miguel E. Santillan
http://santillanstudio.deviantart.com

SECOND EDITION

SPEARTIP PUBLISHING

ISBN 9781980780137

For Alexandros, Reka
and Leonidas, the future King of Sparta.

Special thanks to
Beautiful Fong and Handsome Miguel

Mr. Deathmask

by

Lee McGeorge

"To judge from the notions expounded by theologians, one must conclude that God created most men simply with a view to crowding hell."

- Marquis de Sade

CHAPTER ONE

The electric gates to the estate were closing when Henri Bonheur saw a man slip between them. He almost made it in with absolute stealth, but was caught in the glow of the vehicle's tail-lights. "What the fuck!"

Henri watched in the rear-view mirror. The intruder wore a long coat and a bowler hat. In the blink of an eye he vanished into woodland, but the game was up. He was seen.

Henri mumbled the words, "You mother fucker." He ran the engine slowly, continuing up to the house. There was a hedgerow on one side of the estate with gates set in the middle. The trespasser had not surveyed his target well; he could have walked around the hedge rather than risk slipping in through the gates. "I don't know what you want," Henri muttered. "but you won't like what you find."

The bowler hat jogged a memory. Maybe a week earlier he'd seen it. Where was he? Mayfair perhaps?

Oxford Street? He'd seen someone wear a bowler hat and it stood out in the modern world. He looked carefully in the mirrors, moving his head to widen his field of view. "Where the hell are you?"

The Land Rover pulled into the courtyard between the mansion and game lodge. A security light turned on automatically.

Henri rushed to the game lodge and went straight for the gun cabinet. He took a side-by-side shotgun, loaded it and dropped a few extra shells in his pocket, then pulled up his left sleeve to reveal his mark. It was a burn in the shape of a large hand. Talon like fingers that had wrapped around his forearm to brand his skin; in the centre was a pentagram. A five-pointed star within a circle, raised red against the melted flesh. Henri pressed his lips against the wound. "May the One True Lord protect me."

He went back outside. The security light came on. The intruder was hiding but Henri could sense the man's presence; he was hiding in the forest and Henri followed his intuition and pointed the weapon into the darkness. "You're not sneaking up on me. No fucking way do you sneak up on me."

For a moment, he visualised his own death. It was an image he'd seen a thousand times, laid out naked on silken sheets in his Burgundy chateau. Through his future eyes he watched as his wrinkled hand reached forward. His skin was covered in liver spots and his fingers trembled with a mild palsy. Sitting around him were a half-dozen naked girls who stroked his skin. He was almost a hundred years old and the vision he conjured wouldn't happen for another fifty years. His withered future hand stroked across the exposed breasts of the closest girl; a girl who was yet to be born but was already destined to tend him in his final hours.

Then he realised the vision was different. The light dimmed in the chateau and the girls faces began to sink into their skulls. Their skin was turning grey. The beautiful perfect breasts he was touching crumbled under his fingers as though they were ash. "What is happening?" he whispered. It was his gift. He could look at any man or woman and see how they died. He could even see his own death. But the vision was changing. In his imagination, he spoke out to the girls and asked, "Where are you going?" but the words went unanswered as they dissolved to a grey transparency. He tried to grasp the arm of the closest girl but his fingers sunk into her flesh and she vanished, leaving him with a fist full of ash. "Josephine," he whispered. "Josephine, where are you going?" She was gone. Then he was gone. Then the vision was gone.

What the hell was happening?

The security light clicked off and Henri Bonheur found himself back on his farm with a loaded shotgun pressed to his shoulder. He listened carefully. The woodland always made noise, but he could hear twigs break and leaves rustle and sensed it was more than just nature. This wasn't right. This wasn't possible. The One

True Lord had gifted him with the ability to see death coming, yet now the gift deserted him.

A closer sound, a rustle of leaves. Henri pointed the shotgun and aimed at the noise. "Get inside," he mumbled to himself. "Don't take chances." He moved towards the house, walking backwards, sweeping the shotgun through a shallow arc towards where he felt the intruder was waiting.

Then from the treeline, one of the shadows stepped forward. He was huge; over six feet tall with the width to match. The moonlight traced an outline of his coat and bowler hat.

"I can see you," Henri yelled. "Get off my farm or by fuck I'll blow you in half and feed you to the pigs."

The man took a step forward.

Henri raised the shotgun. "I fucking mean it," he spat. "Go now or I'll shoot you." The bowler-hat-man took another step. "I said fuck off." Henri raised the barrel and fired a high warning shot. The blast shook the treetops and sent roosting birds into a panic. The whole forest came alive with the screeching and scurrying of wildlife.

A breathy sound came from behind. A voice whispered his name, "Henri."

"The fuck?" He spun to see…

"Wh… What?"

"Henri," it said again.

There was a little girl. She wore a white dress and floated three feet off the ground. Her long hair was drifting wildly about her and as the moonlight caught her face she said, "Mister Deathmask has come for you, Henri."

"What the hell?" He raised the shotgun.

"But I want Leonora."

"FUCK YOU!" He fired the gun with perfect aim into the ghost girl's chest making her vanish as simply as turning out the light.

He'd fired his two shots.

The bowler-hat-man charged towards him.

Henri ran.

He made it ten yards before something hit between the shoulders, knocking him to his knees. The shotgun caught the ground and spun out of his hands but he was able to grab the end of the hot barrel and roll, sheer luck keeping the momentum to get him back on his feet. He ran hard, opening the weapon as he went, the shells ejecting with a trail of smoke. He ran for the lodge, then he was pushed again. The knock made him lose his balance and sent him crashing against the door frame.

He turned and swung the shotgun like a club but it was caught and ripped from his hands... He was... his face?

"What the fuck are you?"

His attacker punched fast like a boxer, going in for the kill with lefts and rights, overhand punches that smashed bone and broke teeth. Through the pain, Henri saw the man's fists were embellished with golden metal. Metal that ripped flesh. Metal that crushed his cheekbone and shattered his eye socket.

The attacker wore a mask. A red mask to make him look like a demon of some kind. A long coat. A demon mask. A bowler hat. Metal on his fists.

"What the fuuuuuuck! MY LORD! MY LORD!" Henri screamed out of sheer desperation as he was beaten into complete physical submission. The punches came like hammer blows to smash him into oblivion. Then the attacker stepped back. Henri tried to say, "Please," but little came out other than a slurring drool of blood. "What do you want?"

The attacker said nothing. He pulled something from his hands. Knuckledusters. That's what the metal was. Heavy brass with sharp edges. "I asked, what do you want?" Henri touched his face and brought his hands back covered in blood. His world was spinning. He had no physical or mental ability to defend himself. Where was his God? Where was the One True Lord? "What?" Henri whispered in a slur. "Tell me what you want."

The attacker pulled a short length of hose from his right sleeve. Fluid sprayed across his legs and the smell of petrol was immediate. Oh, Fuck! Henri pressed his arms back to try and roll but a boot kicked solidly into his chest that knocked him back as a flame came to bear. "Please, no. I fucking beg you." The hose sprayed fire, igniting the petrol and turning his legs into a fireball.

Henri bounced to his feet and swatted the flames, dancing on the spot until a punch to the face laid him flat on his back. He screamed shrill and loud, shrieking through panic as much as through pain, patting his legs futilely to try and pound out the fire.

Henri felt like a dying insect; lying on his back, kicking his legs and flapping his arms in futility. It wasn't fair. He couldn't die now, he couldn't. His mission was incomplete. If he died now he'd burn in hell forever. He was supposed to die in France. He was supposed to die surrounded by beautiful young girls. He was supposed to die in fifty years' time.

"I can't die now," were his final coherent words. Then he screamed without the ability to think straight, feeling that each breath he took was counting down to his final one. Then the demon-masked man knelt beside him, gripped his throat and began to crush his larynx with the power of a machine.

He was going to die. There was no preventing it. He stared up at his attacker with a final emotion of incredulity. How could this happen, he thought? How on Earth could you kill me?

----- X -----

The attacker took a step back to view the smouldering corpse. The fabric of Henri Bonheur's trousers had burned away but there was still a small flame on the man's briefs where the fatty tissue of his penis wicked through his underwear.

From within his coat, he took a roll of waxed linen with newspaper backing. He positioned it over Henri

13

Bonheur's broken face and set fire to the corner, the fire spread across the linen diagonally, melting the wax so that it ran into the cracks of a shattered face. A breath of cold wind set the wax in place and, with absolute care, the attacker lifted the mould of Henri Bonheur's shattered face.

----- X -----

Thirty-five years earlier…

In another time, somewhere on the African continent, a young boy had seen an evil that had changed the course of his life. An evil that had opened the doorway for him to become an angel. For him to become, Mister Deathmask.

"Come, child," his mother was saying. She was dragging him through the crowd. The roads were deep-red and made of dirt. His mother wore a colourful dress of green and white, with a matching headdress. All the women wore colourful clothes. The men wore simple slacks and shirts. He, like the other five-year-old boys, wore only shorts and his feet were shoeless. There were hundreds of people and he could already hear them singing.

People were rhythmical hopping from foot to foot and those who knew the songs joined in. "I can't see. Mother, I can't see."

Mother craned her neck to see above the crowd

and grinned. She was already clapping and caught under the spell. Mister Deathmask let go of her hand and crawled through people's legs to get to the front.

The display was magnificent. There were men, dressed as traditional warriors with grass skirts and animal hide trimmings. Their shields were tall and thin, their spears straight and deadly. Around their calves they wore genet's tails and across their biceps and around their head they wore a band of leopard fur.

They danced the dance of the bravest men and chanted with spellbinding ferocity. The drums beat whilst the bystanders stomped and clapped their hands to become part of the performance. The five-year-old boy had found the best seat in the house and sat cross-legged at the front.

He could see it all.

Then a new player came to the stage. A man who was dressed like the warriors but wearing a wooden mask of horror. The face was evil, with savage eyes and a growled smirk and the moment he saw it he felt his blood freeze and his muscles lock rigid.

The drums beat louder and faster.

The brave warriors ran to encircle the devil man as he stomped and leaped into the centre. He kicked his legs high and he waved his arms as the surrounding warriors pointed their spears at him. They chanted and grunted and shuffled in a circular motion, their spear tips closing in on the devil, shooting forward and withdrawing in time with their rhythmical chant. But Mister Deathmask knew what the adults didn't. He knew the man in the centre was really the devil. It wasn't a man in a mask, it was the devil and his real mask was the skin of a warrior. The boy could barely breathe with the realisation. He was watching the devil, pretending to be a man, pretending to be the devil. But nobody else could see. They were too busy clapping and singing to notice the evil amongst them.

Mister Deathmask pressed his little fists to his temples and bit his teeth together. He could feel his nostrils flare as his breathing became rapid and deep. His skin broke out into a feverish sweat whilst his mind tipped over into an almost blind panic. The only thing that was saving him were the brave warriors with their spears and shields. They had the devil surrounded, they had their sharp points pushed close to him. The brave men were keeping the devil at bay. But then the devil pressed his chest to the sky and cried out in a warbling tone that brought the warriors crashing to the floor. They dropped their weapons and either died or fell into a great sleep, but no matter what happened, the devil was now free to approach the crowd. The boy tried to say, "Mother," but the word was trapped in his throat. The devil hissed and pointed his finger at the bystanders. He turned in a circle, looking down his arm as the crowd fell silent and shuffled back slightly.

He was too terrified to move.

The devil was free.

Those who were supposed to keep him at bay were

either dead or sleeping.

Then the devil was looking at him. The devil was pointing at him. The devil was coming towards him.

The young boy's muscles became paralysed. His breathing stopped. His tiny little five-year-old heart clenched in his chest and the world went dark. And in that moment of deepest, most horrifying terror, a doorway was opened. A doorway that only opens when the most innocent know purest horror.

"I am here, little one," said the girl's voice. "I will protect you."

He didn't remember asking her anything out loud, but felt an overwhelming sense of love. His words flowed out through his mind rather than his lips. "Who are you?" he asked.

"I am Magdalena. And we have special work to do, my angel."

----- X -----

Ten years later and the boy was in Tangier…

"What you want, Mister?" he asked. "You want get high? Smoke? Opium? Want fuck nice young girl?" His job was to carry the bags of sailors and those in search of North Africa's unpleasant delights. "I know a place that can give you a nice young girl."

"How about a nice young boy?" the man replied.

"Sir. From babe to schoolboy."

The man was white, with dark stubble, sunken cheeks and a lithe, sinewy build. "You have babies?"

"You want fuck a baby?"

"No," the man said. "I want to eat a baby. A boy."

The fifteen-year-old slowed his pace. "I know a place. But is a big cost and I must speak with them first. But is possible. Do you really want?"

The cannibal's eyes flashed dark. "I want a baby boy that has tasted nothing but its mother's milk."

The teenager carried the man's bags to the hotel and offered to return that evening. He found the man sitting in the bar sipping gin. "A beggar girl has baby today, a boy. She cannot afford to keep baby and has given him to The Marbia. The Marbia will sell you this baby for one thousand American dollars."

The cannibal leaned close. "If you're lying to me," he whispered. "I'll eat you instead."

"I'm not lying, Mister. The Marbia has what you want."

They travelled across the city to the El Mrabet district. Men sat outside cafés smoking shisha pipes. The teenager led the way to a place with no lights. He took the cannibal to an alleyway with only a bad smell. They passed a sick dog with barely the strength to stand, crying and dying from a gangrenous wound to its neck. "Is this way," he said. He opened the door and descended to a cellar lit with candles.

A wrinkled old woman, the Marbia, was dressed in traditional Berber clothing of dark dress and headscarf embellished with golden embroidery. There was a wooden table with a single chair, a traditional jambiya curved knife was to the right and in pride of place, was a one-day-old baby boy asleep on a platter.

The Marbia held out a wrinkled hand with gnarled knuckles. "You pay her now," the boy said. The cannibal handed over a wad of dirty American dollars without taking his eyes from his feast. "I wait outside."

He left the man alone and closed the door, but did not retreat further. He watched through the keyhole as the cannibal removed his linen suit, shirt and underwear. In his hand, he clutched his own jambiya, his palm sweating against the handle. The cannibal was undressing so as not to get blood on his clothing, or maybe to smear the infant's blood across his chest and face. Then he saw the mark. Across his right shoulder was a burned and angry scar of a pentagram within a circle. In his mind, he heard Magdalena speak, "He is one of them," she said. "He can lead us to Leonora."

The cannibal took his seat and picked up the knife in his right hand. With his left, he took hold of the child's ankles and lifted the babe to expose his buttocks. Then he looked up to the ceiling and said aloud, "Hear my praise. I am a servant to the One True Lord and I take this child in his honour."

The cannibal made a slice down the back of the child's leg and into the buttock. The blood of a one-day-old baby spilled across the platter. Within a second, the teenager smashed through the door and rushed the cannibal. With an almost superhuman power he knocked the man from his chair and struck fast with the jambiya, getting the curved blade between the cannibal's ribs and puncturing a lung. Then he swung it to his neck and hit the jugular. Then he stabbed at his face and the blade embedded so deeply into his temple it got stuck in his head.

Behind him the baby cried out in little ack-ack-ack noises. The Marbia came into the room to collect the infant and tend to his wound as Mister Deathmask stepped back to see the dead cannibal laying in a pool of his own spreading blood.

"Well done, my angel," Magdalena whispered. "Well done."

He rolled the man to take a closer look at the mark on his shoulder. "What is it?" he asked.

Magdalena didn't respond.

He washed and changed into the clothes of the cannibal. He went back to the dead man's hotel and searched his belongings. There were documents there, things he couldn't possibly understand as he'd never attended school or learned to read, but he felt a compulsion to take them and head to the port. He took a boat to Spain and travelled North into France then climbed aboard a truck filled with tomatoes and six hiding men to make his way illegally into England. All the way he felt his journey being guided by some force, a unique sensation that walked him into a solicitor's office.

"Can I help you?" The man wore a pinstriped suit,

wire frame glasses and had slicked back hair. The teenager didn't speak, but the solicitor seemed to vaguely recognise him. "Who do you represent?"

"Magdalena. I have these papers."

The official little man took the documents and began sifting through them. "How did you come by these deeds?" he asked. "These papers, where did you get them?"

"I killed a man in Tangier, they were his."

The solicitor leafed through them. "There are some title deeds here, a property you can live in if you wish. I shall take care of the paperwork so that the home belongs to you. It can be sold at any time should you need the money, but you, as Magdalena's representative, shall be the custodian and owner of that property."

Mister Deathmask didn't understand. All he knew was he had done good.

----- X -----

Mister Deathmask carefully carried the mould of Henri Bonheur's face back through the streets of London. The house of the cannibal had looked well-kept when he took it twenty-five years ago. Now it was a wreck. He'd never cut the grass or painted the doors or window frames. He'd never trimmed the privet hedge which hung out into the street. Some of the windows were cracked. Inside were no carpets. The kitchen had a table with two chairs and one of the bedrooms had a mattress on the floor and a blanket. There was electricity but he rarely used it. Electricity felt like a luxury he didn't need.

In the kitchen, he emptied his coat pockets of the brass knuckles and took off his coat to reveal a contraption slung from a holster that he'd fashioned from two leather belts. It was a vintage atomiser for spraying water onto plants. Made from brass, the cylinder was the size and shape of a small fire-extinguisher. On one end was a pump handle and on the other a hose that ran the length of his arm. In its time, a gardener could fill the cylinder with water, pump up the pressure and spray the water. He used it with petrol that could spray from a hose in his sleeve.

He placed a box of sand on the table and scooped out a hollow into which he carefully placed the mould of Henri Bonheur's face.

Plaster of Paris was mixed.

He poured carefully.

He sat for hours watching it dry.

He watched the sun rise. He heard the dawn chorus. He waited until ten in the morning before testing the plaster with a light touch to ensure it had dried. Then with the greatest of care, he upended the box of sand and removed the mould and its precious cargo.

The death mask came away easily.

Henri Bonheur's cast had even copied his smashed teeth. Every wrinkle of his lips. The lop-sidedness of his face from the broken jaw. The deep slices into his skin. The distortions of his broken eye socket. Everything was preserved. He had captured the scream of a gifted man dying before his mission was complete.

Carrying the facsimile of Henri Bonheur, he went upstairs to the front bedroom. The trophy room. On one wall were death masks of two women and a young boy. On another wall were six death masks, all men. All of them were screaming.

----- X -----

He broke six eggs into a dirty coffee mug and drank them all in one go, raw. Stripped naked, he exercised in the front room of the home. One hundred push-ups against bare floorboards. One hundred tricep dips between two chairs. Two hundred abdominal crunches.

He cleared away the chairs and stood in a boxer's stance, throwing rapid lefts and rights in combination. Then he took to visualising an opponent in front of him and practiced the moves to grab his foe and snap their neck. He practiced with a knife, imagining stabbing somebody and immediately twisting the blade. If the time ever came to murder with a blade his muscle memory would ensure his thrusts were death strikes.

After an hour of exertion, his skin was covered in beads of sweat and his breathing was rapid. Now it was time to stretch and work on flexibility with a series of yoga poses. He allowed the sweat to dry on him which would add to the already potent smell of sebum. He prayed for a while, sitting crossed legged in the front room. He was unsure where his prayers were directed. He wasn't a believer in dogmatic religion but somehow felt compelled to commune with the universe. One thing he did believe is if there was a God, he was a terrifying God; but the good news is he was part of that God's plan.

----- X -----

As the sky darkened Mister Deathmask felt Magdalena's presence drawing closer. He brought the cast of Henri Bonheur back to the kitchen and lit candles as he waited.

She was coming. He could feel it.

"I am waiting, Magdalena. Are you with me?"

"Yes." The voice of the little girl came as a hollow whisper.

Tears of joy welled in his eyes. "I have the face of Mister Foresight for you."

"I know," the voice whispered. "I was with you last night. Did you see me?"

Mister Deathmask wiped his eyes with his sleeve. "Yes."

From behind, a ghostly form materialised and drifted past, her hair and dress flowing. At first glance she looked like smoke, but as she moved the ghost solidified into a human shape, then further into the outline of a little girl before forming fully solid as a child of six or seven years old. Her bare feet walked across the wooden floorboards to the table.

Mister Deathmask gently took hold of her hands

and placed them on the cast of Henri Bonheur.

"Ah yes," she whispered. "Mister Foresight." Her hands traced the lines of his face, her tiny little fingers traced the lips and felt the jagged edges of his broken teeth. "He made so many victims I can barely count; but you have stopped him, my angel. You have done masterful work."

"Thank you," Deathmask replied. "There are more. He has friends. I know how to find them. I can kill them all. I can kill them in their lair when they are together."

"No, my love." The little girl reached out and touched his face, her fingers feeling the tears across his cheek. "You will kill them slowly. You will torment them until they are maddened and confused. That is when they will call upon Leonora and that is when we will kill them."

Deathmask's face scrunched with emotion, his smile widened whilst his eyes closed to squeeze out a few more tears. Magdalena moved closer and kissed him, then backed away so he could look at her childish face.

It was an abomination.

Where her eyes should have been, there were two bleeding dark holes.

"I love you," he whispered. "And I will punish her for taking your eyes."

With that, Magdalena began to fade. Her legs and arms first, then her torso, until all that was left was her eyeless face floating in the air. Her damaged face. Her pretty childish face with bleeding eye holes. They had blinded the child in a dark blessing. Who could do such a thing? What kind of person could take such innocence and cut out her eyes?

Mister Deathmask knew; and Mister Deathmask was going to make them suffer.

CHAPTER TWO

Andrew Bray was using the first light for a quick run before work. He pounded the streets through Stoke Newington and entered Abney Park Cemetery where he had a favourite route that took him along every pathway. The burial ground was a favourite place for street drinkers and rock-band photoshoots.

He saw a girl between the headstones, then noticed the two men watching her. She was slumped awkwardly, wearing a black leather jacket. Even at this early hour the men were drinking from cans of lager. At first, he thought the men were having bad ideas on what to do with an unconscious girl, but on a second glance he registered the worry in their faces.

"Is she alright?" He asked whilst jogging on the spot.

"I don't know," the street drinker said with an East European accent. "We see her only now."

Andrew stepped amongst the headstones. "Hey," he called. "Hey, young lady, are you okay?" Up close he could see the girl had a tattoo on her neck, a playing card of the ace of spades. He patted her shoulder but got no response. He tried shaking her and got the same result.

27

Stepping more carefully between the gravestones, he put his hand against her cheek and felt how cold she was. "Oh, shit." He was involved now. He hadn't wanted to be, but the situation meant the girl needed an ambulance. She was ice cold, unconscious and unresponsive. He turned back to the drinkers and asked, "Can one of you call an ambulance. Tell them we've found an unconscious girl."

"I have no credit on phone," the first man answered dismissively.

"You don't need credit, just call nine-nine-nine."

The men discussed something in their Slavic tongue.

"Guys? Please, you need to call an ambulance."

The second drinker spoke up, "He doesn't want to call because he is illegal."

"Illegal?"

"Immigrant. I don't want trouble with police."

Andrew stood up not sure how to demand they help him. "Please. Look at me, I was out running, I don't have my phone."

The drinker pointed to his leg. "You cut yourself."

He looked down to see his right leg covered in blood from his knee to his foot. He wiped at it. He checked himself. He wasn't bleeding. It was the girl. Andrew lifted her arm and saw blood falling everywhere. "Holy fuck! She's bleeding. She's bleeding bad. Guys. Call for an ambulance."

"I don't want trouble," the man replied. "I'm

illegal. I don't want trouble."

Andrew found the source of the bleeding, her wrist was severed. He held her hand high, putting pressure on the wound. "Come on guys, I need…"

They were walking away.

"No… Guys? Fellas? I need you to call an ambulance… Oh shit… Help! HELP! HELP! ANYBODY. HELP!"

----- X -----

The paramedics lifted the girl onto a gurney and were holding her bleeding wrist high. One of them found a purse in her pocket and handed it to the watching policeman. The street drinkers were coming out in force and there were at least two dozen of life's forgotten losers watching the scene unfold.

The policeman went through the purse. "It says her name is Nicola Bannister."

"Nicola, can you hear me," the paramedic shouted. "Nicola. Open your eyes." He waited a second then yelled it and twisted the skin by her collar bone. "I SAID OPEN YOUR EYES!"

The girl didn't move or respond but the blood and pulse monitor clipped to her finger were showing that she was still alive. Barely.

"We've got to move fast," the paramedic said.

----- X -----

Doctor Peter Hill felt the familiar sexual tightening in his groin as he read the email. "Thank goodness you're still alive, Nikki. I wouldn't want you to die without me." He ran his fingers through his hair and pressed his shoulders back to improve his posture before making the call. "Good morning, I'm trying to reach Doctor Christodoulou. My name is Doctor Peter Hill, I'm calling from..."

"...Yes, Doctor Hill, I am Christodoulou, thank you for getting in touch so quickly. I have one of your service users who was brought in as a failed suicide attempt. Her name is Nicola Bannister."

Doctor Hill tried to maintain his professionalism but couldn't quite stop himself smirking. "I received your message. What condition is she in? Physically and mentally?"

"Physically, she is stable. Mentally, I would describe her as being subdued. She's tearful and worries she's being a burden. We saw from her records that she was being treated by you for compound depressive illness. I was hoping you could give me some background. We want to talk to her about what she's done, but I don't want to put her in an emotionally difficult place, anything you can offer would be helpful."

"We've been treating her on and off for two years. She suffered a family tragedy when her younger brother was murdered at only five years old whilst she was supervising him."

"My goodness."

"She was fifteen at the time and took her baby brother, Callum, to her local park. The boy wandered off, or was taken. One moment he was there and the next he was missing. She raised the alarm but he was found murdered and the case was never solved."

At the other end of the phone the doctor made a long humming noise. "I see."

Beneath his desk, Doctor Hill stroked his manhood through his trousers. "Nicola, Nikki as she prefers to be called, blames herself. After the murder, her step-father, who was Callum's biological father, abandoned Nikki and her mother; then within months Nikki's mother died from extreme alcohol abuse."

The other doctor hummed again. "Ordinarily we would admit her to inpatient psychiatric care," he said, "But the closest bed is in Buckinghamshire. Physically, she is well enough to leave, but she clearly requires psychological treatment. As you already have a rapport and history, would it be better if you continued her treatment?"

Doctor Hill rubbed his groin a little more. "We could take her as an outpatient. That might work. I'd like to see Nikki again." He could feel himself becoming erect. "I'd very much like to see Nikki again."

With the call ended, Doctor Hill checked behind him to ensure he was alone, then pulled up his trouser leg and reached down to stroke the pentagram scar on the back of his right calf. "I thank you, Lord, for this blessing. I thank you for bringing me such playthings."

----- X -----

"Easy Jez, easy." Maxine Elsworth pulled the reigns tight on Jezebel. There was a police car approaching the cottage. It was a wet morning with a low hanging mist that made the green fields fade into grey. The horse snorted and stomped her feet. "What is this, Jez?" Maxine's farmhouse bordered woodland to the rear and paddocks either side. She was half a mile from the main road giving her all the seclusion a privacy-minded woman could want.

The police car crept up the driveway and Maxine brought the horse to bear, looking down onto a youthful looking policeman with blonde hair. "Good morning," he said. "I'm looking for Maxine Elsworth."

"I'm Miss Elsworth." Jezebel stomped her feet uneasily. "Give me a moment to stable her." The horse snorted breaths of hot air and stomped in agitation at the intruder in her paddock. "It's okay Jez," Maxine whispered as she dismounted. "I know you hate men." With the animal stabled, Maxine returned to her visitor. "How can I help?"

"I'm afraid there's been a death in the area and we're having some trouble finding relatives to identify the remains." The policeman was in his early twenties, he fidgeted without making eye contact. "You may want to prepare yourself, Miss Elsworth."

"Alright."

"We believe the man who has died is a friend of

yours. Henri Bonheur."

Maxine laughed, then caught herself and clapped a hand over her mouth. "You're wrong. Henri is fine."

The policeman made a slight grimace. "I'm afraid I need to ask for your help. We need to identify the remains. If you could help us it would be much appreciated."

With her hands on her hips, Maxine stared off to the side and grit her teeth. "So stupid," she mumbled.

"Miss Elsworth?"

"I said this is stupid," she snapped. "Henri is fine."

"No, Ma'am, I don't believe he is. And we really need your help."

----- X -----

"Are we not going to the hospital?" Maxine asked.

"We're going to a private mortician. In the event of a suspicious death, remains are taken to a private undertaker."

"A suspicious death?" Maxine shook her head, "This whole thing is a waste of my time." She snorted a laugh at the thought. Henri may have killed somebody but he wasn't dead.

The car pulled in at a small cottage with a glossy black sign that read Ives and Sons, Funeral Directors. The undertaker's premises were on a village high street of little traffic, directly opposite was a rising hill that looked like a road to nowhere. She steadied herself and gazed at a dark blue car parked on the hill. There was a big, black man sitting behind the wheel. He was unmoving. He was watching. Maxine focussed her eyesight more attentively. It seemed out of place.

"Please come inside." It was the director, Andrew Ives, an old professional man with silver hair and permanent solemnity. Maxine broke her gaze and followed the undertaker through a small lounge and into a white-tiled room with yellow biohazard stickers on the wall. This was the other side of the funeral business. An embalming area that looked vaguely like a restaurant kitchen and smelled of a chemistry lab.

"I'm afraid the deceased has facial injuries," he said. "I wanted to forewarn you." Ives opened the door to a walk-in cold-room and pulled out a gurney covered in a blue sheet. "Are you prepared?"

Maxine shrugged. The sheet was pulled back and… "FUCK ME… Holy fuck it IS Henri!" She grabbed the policeman's wrist and yelled, "Come with me." The constable followed her like a child as she marched him to the lounge, slamming the door behind her. She turned to face him and lifted his clenched wrist ahead of his eyes. "Get on your knees you stupid, fucking, imbecile." The policeman lowered himself into a position of subservience. "Now listen to me you little cunt," she began. "You're going to tell me every detail the police have on this. The One True Lord demands it."

The policeman had turned an ashen colour and in a weak voice mouthed, "Yes, Ma'am."

Mister Deathmask

----- X -----

Mister Deathmask watched the woman drag the policeman out behind her. She was stomping her feet as she walked and pulling the officer about by his wrist like he was a naughty toddler. "She is gifted," Mister Deathmask mumbled to himself. "She has touch on him."

From his vantage point, he could not hear what was being said, but it was clear the woman had absolute physical control over the man.

"Can you see this, Magdalena? She is servant to The Disease."

The woman was commanding the policeman back into the car. She got in herself and the vehicle moved out. Deathmask started the car engine to follow but felt a ghostly presence hold him in place.

Magdalena wanted him to wait.

----- X -----

The candlestick chart was set to one minute bars. Today, Jason Kinnear was looking at the value of the Euro. How many Euros bought how many American Dollars.

"Hey, Jason." A voice from the doorway, "I heard you were shorting the Euro. Is that true?" The kid was Martin Blake. Barely out of university and full of enthusiasm.

"Yes. Just waiting for an entry."

"I only ask because I'm trading long and I want to know if there's something I've missed. Everybody I know is giving it a ninety percent chance of rising."

Jason kept his eyes on the screen. "That means there's a ten percent chance of it falling."

"So why go short? Why bet it falls if it's more likely to rise?"

"I'm short for the fat tail exposure." Jason executed the trade, selling Euros at ten thousand pounds per pip. The Euro gained ten pips in value and he was losing a hundred grand within seconds. "If the Euro rises my losses will be small and manageable. But if it falls, I'll make a fortune."

The candlestick flickered between red and green. He expected to see a lot of red on the screen in the next hour. He knew it was going to happen; they didn't call him Mister Market for nothing. The telephone rang. "Jason Kinnear speaking."

"Jason, it's Maxine."

"Maxine, this is a work line, it's recorded. Can you call me on my mobile when…"

"…Henri has been killed," she shouted. "Oh, fuck. Jason. Mister Foresight is dead. He was murdered." Jason felt his stomach turn a somersault.

"That can't happen, Maxine. It's not possible."

"I'm sitting in a police car right now, they brought me to a fucking mortuary to see the remains. Mister Foresight was murdered last night. Somebody smashed him to fucking pieces."

"It can't be," he said weakly. "Tell me what happened. Step by step, explain it."

"The police came to my home. They said Henri had died and they needed me to identify the remains." Maxine laid out the history lucidly and calmly.

Jason rested his elbows on the table and propped up his head with a hand to his forehead. "I need to finish something here then I'll come to you. I'll leave London within the hour and head to your home. I'd like to see Henri's body. I'd like to see this for myself."

"Come quickly." She hung up.

Jason walked to the window. From the high floors of One Canada Square he could see right across London. Ordinarily he enjoyed this view. It felt good to look down on the worthless at street level. On occasion, he fantasised about pissing on them from this high vantage. He made a fist and lightly hit it on the window.

"Is something wrong?" Martin asked.

"Oh… just a… yeah…"

No. It couldn't be.

It just wasn't possible.

The One True Lord had blessed Mister Foresight. Henri's job was to keep them all alive until their mission was complete. Without him death could come at any moment and they… oh fuck… Oh FUCK!

Jason returned to his trading screen and exited the position. Two hundred and twenty three pips down, just as his gift had told him. He'd made two million, two hundred and thirty thousand pounds within minutes.

Normally he would have taken the rest of the day off, maybe pick up a few truant schoolgirls and introduce them to cocaine.

Henri Bonheur was dead, yet he was the one man death couldn't approach.

----- X -----

Jason Kinnear pulled his Aston Martin out of the parking bay then stopped to send a text message. 'Henri killed. Call urgent.'

It was during work hours and he expected the doctor to be busy, but to his relief the phone rang immediately. "Henri killed?" The voice was jovial. "What's the punchline?"

"It's not a joke. Maxine called to say Mister Foresight has been killed. I find it hard to believe and I'm heading over to check myself. Do you want to come with me?"

There was a long pause. "You're fucking kidding me, right?"

"I'm deadly serious, brother. Maxine has identified the remains, but I just can't bring myself to believe without seeing for myself. If you want to come with me, I can pick you up in ten minutes."

----- X -----

Doctor Peter Hill put down the phone and slumped into

his chair. "Not possible. It's just not possible."

As he said it, the junior psychiatrist, Doctor Luke Edwards, came into the office. "Something wrong?"

Doctor Hill reached behind him and rubbed the back of his right calf. If the younger doctor wasn't there he would have rolled up his trouser leg to touch his pentagram scar directly. "Yes, something is wrong."

Luke pulled tissue from a dispenser and began cleaning his glasses. "Do I need to know about it?"

"No, it's a personal issue… Yes, actually, yes there is something that concerns you… I'm sorry I've just been thrown by some unfortunate news. I need to go out for the rest of the day. Can you have reception reschedule my appointments?"

Luke took a seat. "I can do that."

Peter Hill tore a note from a pad and passed it over. "This is what concerns you. I wanted to deal with her myself but I know you have rapport with this girl. Nicola Bannister, do you remember her?"

"Nikki, yes. What about her?"

"Suicide attempt. She's at Homerton Uni after slashing her wrist."

Luke squeezed his eyes closed. "Oh, no. She was doing really well."

"You need to speak with the staff at Homerton; they don't have psychiatric space and want to transfer her to us as an outpatient."

"After a suicide attempt? Surely she needs inpatient care?"

Doctor Hill shrugged. "True, but they just don't have the beds and we have a history with her. I want you to bring her in and make an assessment for future care."

Luke sighed. "Such a shame. Yes. I'll take care of that. Leave her with me."

----- X -----

Maxine's hands trembled. She clenched her left hand in her right fist. As the policeman dropped her back at the cottage he said, "If you need help we would recommend you contact a bereavement counselling service."

"Fuck off!" Maxine slammed the car door and didn't look back. The idiot policeman had said far more than he should have and was undoubtedly in confusion as to why he'd got to his knees and spilled so much information.

In the cottage, she opened her blouse and stood ahead of the hallway mirror. The burned scar of the pentagram visible from the top of her bra cup. "Are you still with me? I give myself to you, my Lord. Please, are you still with me?"

There was no answer.

She poured a scotch and drank it quickly. She poured another and made the next phone call.

"Marigold? Marigold, it's Maxine."

The voice at the other end spoke with the usual sweetness. "Yes, Dear, how are you?"

"Marigold, listen. Mister Foresight has been

killed."

There was a long pause. "Are you sure?"

Maxine swallowed another mouthful and wiped her lips with the back of her hand. "I've just identified his body. He was smashed to a pulp and set on fire." She pressed her hand under her bra to rest the palm against the pentagram

"Who else knows about this?"

"I called Jason, he's coming over because he wants to see the body himself." She let herself fall back into the chair. "Oh, Marigold, I don't know what to think."

"What do you know for sure? Tell me what happened. How did you discover this?"

Maxine sipped on the whisky and relayed the story.

"Did you put your hands on anybody?" the old woman asked. "Did you use your gift? Did you control anybody?"

"Yes. A policeman. He told me a delivery driver had discovered a body on Henri's farm and made a nine-nine-nine call. He said the police believe the body had been there overnight but he didn't know why they suspected that."

"What are the police doing now?"

"I don't know." Maxine held the glass of Scotch against her forehead and closed her eyes. "Poor Mister Foresight. He'll be suffering. Won't he?"

"Yes. He will. His mission is incomplete."

"What do we do, Marigold? What do we do when the One True Lord cannot protect us?"

41

"Now, now, Dear. Don't think like that, not yet." Maxine sniffed a little and found herself weeping, it was a long time since she'd cried. "And hush those tears. We're not done yet. Let Jason confirm what you have seen already. Then we shall make The Circle and decide our future actions." Maxine nodded but didn't speak. The old lady changed the subject slightly. "Maxine, when did you last visit me? When did you last come to the manor house?"

She wiped her eyes with the back of her hand then put it back on the pentagram above her breast. "I don't know. A few months."

"Well, I have a very beautiful new twink I'd like you to break in. Finish your business with Jason and then come over this evening around seven and enjoy your privilege. We'll get to the bottom of what happened to Mister Foresight and we will complete our mission. The One True Lord will protect us and everything will be fine, I promise you. But for tonight, let's put our worries aside and have some 'ladies-time'. Yes?"

Maxine sniffed. "Okay," she said. "I would like that."

"Then it's settled. I'll see you tonight at seven."

Marigold Upperton ended her call and took a seat in the hall. She was surrounded by the aftermath of a Women's Institute meeting. Leftover cakes and scones were to be cleared away and only herself and the organiser, a fifty-year-old spinster called Alice remained. "For hell's sake," she mumbled.

"Is something wrong, Marigold?"

"I'm not sure." She heard an unexpected tone of resignation to her own voice. "A strange phone call. Unexpected news."

Alice put scones into a plastic container. "Nothing bad, I hope?"

Marigold went to the door. "Nothing I can't handle." She checked the corridor was clear then closed the door and pressed her back to it, staring at Alice.

The spinster continued clearing away until the nature of Marigold's pose began to feel awkward. "Are you sure there's nothing wrong?"

"Oh, I'm quite sure. There's just something I wanted to talk to you about. Privately."

"Yes?"

Marigold pushed herself away from the door and walked to Alice with a little more swagger and confidence than was customary. She had an appearance modelled after Agatha Christie's Miss Marple; with grey hair kept neat and fine clothes of light greys, puce and mauve. She played the part of an old village lady to perfection, except now, when away from public view and the more confident woman emerged. "I need to show you something. I have a mark on my body."

"What kind of mark?"

Marigold tossed aside her jacket and began

unbuttoning her blouse. "Sit down, please. It's easier to show you if you sit." Alice took a seat but did so slowly, the unusual nature of the situation reading in her face. Marigold pulled her blouse open to reveal large breasts in fine lingerie and a branded pentagram on her flank. The angry burn formed a six-inch-wide circle with five pointed star. "Look at it, Alice. Look right at it."

"Oh, my God." The woman trembled almost instantly.

"Don't say, God."

"Marigold, it's… Oh, it's giving me feelings… What is it?"

"It's my mark. It means I'm chosen. I'm special." Marigold looked down across her breasts to the Women's Institute organiser. "I'd like you to join me Alice."

"Join you with what?" The woman was mesmerised by the symbol. Her breath was slow and deep and her face was flushed with blood.

"Give me your hands."

Alice reached forward and placed her hands in Marigold's, who in turn rested them against her skin, either side of the pentagram. "Tell me what it is."

"There is a Prince coming to our world, Alice. And I am here to help make that happen. But he needs help. The Prince will need a legion of helpers. He will need people like you. People who will give themselves to him."

Alice caressed Marigold's skin, keeping the pentagram between her hands. "Why am I feeling like this?"

"Because you are wanted. Not everybody can feel what you feel. If you had seen my mark and not felt this way I would have been obliged to murder you; but I had a good feeling you were the right sort of woman."

"Oh, God, Marigold."

"Don't say, God."

"Marigold… can I kiss it."

"Do you promise to obey me?"

Alice licked her lips and panted the words, "Oh, yes. Please, Marigold. I've never felt like this in my life. Why? What is happening? What is happening to me?"

"You're being selected. You will have a role in the Prince's congregation. You must hold the secret for now. There will be difficult tasks for you to help me with."

"I'll do anything, Marigold. Please... I want to… do you wish me to become a lesbian?"

"No."

"I will, Marigold. I will do anything."

"Are you sure you'll do anything?" Marigold placed her hands on her hips and held a power pose. Her legs were slightly apart, her open blouse let her breasts raise and her head was held high.

Alice moved off the chair to her knees and brought her face to the mark on Marigold's flank. "What do you want me to do?"

"The bones of babies. I need the bones of new born children."

"Do you mean… real, babies? Like, young

children?"

"Yes. I want you to find within yourself some hatred. I want you to think of what you despise and focus that rage on finding me the bones of new born babies."

"I know a girl who is loose. She's white but has abased herself with black men. Her children are all half-breeds. Can they be used? She lives near me. She has a half-cast baby. I could try and steal it. I'll kill it, it's not a problem."

"That's very good, Alice. Very good indeed. Yes, take this baby and kill it. Then I'll tell you what to do next."

----- X -----

Mister Deathmask was slumped in his car seat, drumming his fingers on the steering wheel. Boredom had set in hours ago and now the sun was going down he was unsure why he was still here.

A car pulled up at the undertakers. A silver Aston Martin.

Mister Deathmask watched as two men got out of the car. "Mister Market," he said aloud. He shook away his fatigue, shuffled in the chair and straightened his back. There was another man with Mister Market, he had salt and pepper hair and a handsome, professional quality. "Is he the doctor? Is he, Merry Murder?" Mister Deathmask watched intently, his body fixed rigid, his eyes wide open. "I see you," he whispered. "I know who you are, Merry Murder. I know what you do; and now I see you."

The men entered the undertakers.

Mister Deathmask waited for at least twenty minutes until they returned. The sun was dying and in the gloom the men gave off a delicate blue aura; a glow that was invisible to most people, but a glow that Mister Deathmask could see.

The Aston Martin pulled away.

Mister Deathmask started the car and began following from a distance; he would follow the doctor and discover his home. "You are weak men. I will come for you. And for the glory of Magdalena, I will kill you."

CHAPTER THREE

Marigold opened the door to find Maxine with her shoulders sagging. "My dear, you look fraught with worry. I won't have it. Come inside."

As Maxine stepped in, Marigold wrapped her arms around her and felt Maxine return the embrace. "I was so glad you invited me. I couldn't bare being alone tonight."

"And I'm glad you came, too. I was beginning to think you weren't coming." She walked Maxine to the kitchen. "Would you like a drink? I was about to have a Bombay and tonic." Without waiting for a response, she began making two drinks. "I need to change. The boy-toys are by the pool if you want to go through, or you can wait for me."

"I'll wait."

Marigold smiled, her head tilted slightly. "Very well, Dear. Let's go upstairs."

The master bedroom had a beautiful large bed and decor of creams and golds. Hanging from a clothes rack was a Salvation Army uniform. Maxine ran her finger along the silver Major badge on the epaulet. "This uniform always reminds me of the Nazi's."

Marigold scoffed. "Oh, those God-bothering

fucktards will be the death of me." She unfastened her skirt and let it fall to the floor. "Still, they're worthwhile. I've converted over twenty of them." She slipped off her jacket and began unfastening her blouse. "I'm currently working on a Women's Institute group and they're a pushover. Those little old ladies harbour some vicious fantasies. It's amazing how twisted people become when they don't exercise their carnal desires. They bottle up their sexual frustrations until they're ready to burst."

"Did you speak with Jason?"

"Yes. He told me the same as yourself, albeit a little more graphically." Marigold moved in a way that flaunted her sexuality. Despite being in her sixties, her long legs, swollen breasts and flat stomach would excite a man of any age.

Maxine's head dipped lower. "Henri will be burning. Right now, as we talk, Henri will be in hell burning."

Marigold unfastened her bra and paused to run her fingers across the pentagram on her flank. "If what we were led to believe is true then yes, he will be burning. But, we were also led to believe we were protected."

Defeated and without an ounce of enthusiasm Maxine mumbled, "The One True Lord protects."

"Oh, hush now, with this sadness." Marigold reached her hand to lift Maxine's chin. "The One True Lord does protect us. And if he failed to protect Henri there might be a good reason for it."

"I suppose."

Marigold went back to undressing. "I have more to worry about than you, I'm, what? Twenty? Twenty-five years older than you? Old age brings me closer to a natural death, yet I don't worry about where we are with the mission. We will both live to bring the Prince to this world. If something happened to Mister Foresight whilst under protection of the One True Lord then there was probably a reason for it. But look, let's not dwell on it for this evening."

Marigold opened her wardrobe and took out a black leather body-harness. She stepped into it, fitting the leather straps and steel hoops around her hips and breasts. She buckled the collar around her neck then pulled on black rubber gloves past her elbows. She brought out matching rubber stockings and began rolling them on.

"Did you say you had a new twink?"

"Yes; and he has a huge cock."

"Where did you find him?"

"He was making movies. He says he's only gay-for-pay, but I know he likes it. He is just so beautiful I had to have him. Eighteen years old and with such a lovely hairless body, you would think he was still a boy. Marigold brought out a ten-inch black rubber dildo and fixed it to her fetish harness.

Finally, she wound up her hair and tucked it beneath the cap of a horned head-dress. The horns reached high and twisted, giving her the look of Maleficent from Sleeping Beauty. The old lady had transformed from a quiet village retiree into a horned sex-bitch with a massive black cock. In this guise she called herself by her special name. Now, she was The Maitresse Bathory. "How do I look?" she asked.

Maxine smiled at the dildo. "You're going to do one of them an injury with that."

"I hope so, Dear. That's what it's for."

----- X -----

The Maitresse Bathory's heels clicked against the floor of the swimming pool as she sauntered in wearing a leather body harness, horns on her head, a big black cock from her groin and a gin and tonic in her hand. "Come over here, boys." Three men, wearing only black rubber shorts, crossed to her. Two looked to be in their thirties whilst the third was much younger. She pointed them out to Maxine. "George and Rupert, you already know," she said with a wave of the hand. "But Andrew is the one I was telling you about. He has a nice, big cock."

Maxine smirked, "I'd like to see that."

The boy began pulling down his shorts, to which The Maitresse yelled, "I didn't tell you to get it out, you fucking pervert."

Andrew lowered his head. "Sorry," he whispered.

"Sorry what?"

"I'm sorry, Maitresse Bathory."

"You need to be fucking sorry." The Maitresse clenched her jaw and breathed hard through her nose.

"You need to learn who is your master, young Andrew."

The boy lowered his head even deeper. "I am sorry, Maitresse."

To Maxine she said, "I'm afraid he's not fully broken in yet."

"Apparently not. But you were right, he's quite cute."

Marigold snapped her fingers at one of the men. "George, pull Andrew's shorts down and show Maxine his cock." The man got to work, rolling down the black rubber shorts to reveal the man-boy's manhood; a nice eight inches of uncut beauty.

"Oh, impressive." Maxine said. "Is it wrong that my first desire was to cut it off?"

The Maitresse Bathory laughed out loud. "Eventually we will. But it will be George who is castrated first. Maybe even tonight. His prick doesn't work anymore so there's no reason we can't geld him."

"Does it still not work?" Maxine asked with an air of surprise.

The Maitresse shook her head and turned her lips to a theatrical frown. "It never worked again."

Maxine put her drink aside and rested her palm on Andrew's chest to feel his muscles. "Does he know what happens if he doesn't please?"

"Oh, yes. He knows what I did to George."

Maxine walked around the young man and whispered in his ear. "Do you know what The Maitresse did to George?"

"Yes," he whispered.

"What did she do?"

"She crushed his testicles with pliers."

"That's right. She crushed them until they burst. They popped like squeezed plums. And then I took hold of his hand and made him eat his own shit. Do you know why?"

"Because he ran away," Andrew said.

"That's right. He ran away. He was disobedient. So, The Maitresse had to go and find him. Did you know that The Maitresse can find anybody?"

"Yes."

"Yes, she can," Maxine reiterated. "So, if you ever run away she will find you and she'll bring you back and she will hurt you beyond any pain you can imagine."

"Yes, Madam."

"Yes," Maxine said smirking. "Yesssss. And do you know why we do this?"

The boy swallowed hard and gasped a few breaths. "No, Madam."

"Because we hate men. We really fucking hate you all."

----- X -----

The traffic moved at a snail's pace. The rain was lashing and the forecast even predicted snow, yet the cyclist trying to squeeze between Mister Market's car and a bus was wearing skin-tight shorts. "Watch the car," he mumbled as the handlebars touched the paintwork. There was a scraping noise as the cyclist ran out of room. "I said watch the fucking car." Bicycle-Man couldn't hear. "Fucking stupid people." The way he felt right now he was tempted to crush Bicycle-Man beneath his wheels.

Mister Foresight was burning.

It was Mister Foresight's job to establish the global church. Whilst the Prince would emerge in London, he would need followers globally. But rules were rules and if you died before the mission was complete, The One True Lord would burn you for your failure. "Sad to see you go, Henri," he whispered. "But now I have to pick up the slack."

From the outside, Almassy House was a ten-storey glass fronted building, whilst the partnership that owned it occupied only a small part of the ground floor, the rest of the building was leased out to more prominent law firms and hot-shot lawyers.

He went to the end office; the one with no windows and a simple brass plate reading Almassy Partners. There were two mahogany desks and the walls were lined with bookcases. It was tidy. It was simple. At a bookcase filled with legal texts, he whispered, "I am a servant of the One True Lord and I bid my entry to his home." He pulled the bookcase outward to reveal a secret staircase. The first steps were neatly edged, but once he descended and turned the first corner, the masonry gave way to something more original. The steps became rough stone blocks and the angle steepened.

He descended further. The width of the passageway grew tighter and more uneven as the natural cave passage arched overhead. Light came from golden bulbs on a string that lit the way deeper and deeper around twisting turns to the secret cave.

It took three or four minutes to reach the bottom and the final door to the inner sanctum. He was the last to arrive.

The cave was at least two hundred feet in length and illuminated with golden lights that showed off the natural rock. At one end was a library area of hand-written grimoires with comfortable reading chairs, currently occupied by Merry Murder, The Maitresse Bathory and The Hands.

Away from the library, was a glass table with executive chairs. Seated here was Kenyan born, Grace Chelimo, also known as Sentinel; and the disgustingly obese, Charles Peachtree, more commonly known as The Pain. The final member of their group was Professor Richard Tudor, known to all as Mister Monoxide.

"You have arrived," the professor said. From a medical breathing mask he took an inhalation of deadly carbon-monoxide gas carried in a small, pressurised bottle. "How are things in the world of finance?"

"As boring as Christianity when you know the outcome. I'm more concerned about how we're going to continue Henri's work."

"Indeed, this is a worry."

"I don't know what worries me more; that Mister

Foresight was killed or that we now have to fulfil his obligation along with our own."

Mister Monoxide made a slow nod. He had a face of lines and ridges suggesting a man in his sixties, but a head of light blonde hair, close-cut and youthful. He wore penny-lens spectacles and bore a passing resemblance to the dramatist, Samuel Beckett; albeit a similarity that was broken whenever he sucked poison gas through a medical mask. "Sentinel has already done some digging into Henri's death," the professor said. "He was burned and beaten, but the police think the cause of death was strangulation."

The Maitresse Bathory called across from the library, "Are you discussing, Henri? If you are then I suggest we make the circle."

They moved to the table, taking their places. One chair was empty.

Maxine Elsworth placed brass goblets and topped each with a dark wine. The Maitresse Bathory began the meeting with a prayer.

"Ave Satana.

Hail, to the One True Lord.
God of our flesh,
God of our minds,
God of our will.
Hail to He who invites us to become as gods.
Bearer of true Light.

O mighty Lord,
teach us to become strong and wise
That we may continue your work in this realm.

Rege Satana."

They raised their goblets and said in unison, "Rege Satana."

The Maitresse Bathory was first to speak. "We are here because Mister Foresight has died a violent death. Murder. Yet we all know this is impossible."

"Not impossible," Mister Monoxide said. "But terrifying if it's true."

"It is true," Jason added. "Merry Murder and I saw with our own eyes. We saw the blessed mark around his arm." He clasped his left wrist and held it up to show exactly where he'd seen the pentagram. "There is only one thing that could do that."

"A Son of Light," Mister Monoxide said.

The loathsome and gelatinous shape that was Charles Peachtree spoke through vocal chords saturated in body fat. "We should be careful not to speak this out loud; otherwise we must summon The Secretary."

"And if we summon The Secretary she will kill one of us," Maxine added with a burst of urgency. "And if we die…"

"…If we die we burn in hell," Mister Monoxide spoke over her. "We know that. We know. The Sons of

Light exist only to destroy our work. If he is here it is to prevent the return of The Prince and must be reported to the Secretary."

"But there are only seven of us," Maxine added. It's Russian Roulette. The Secretary, will murder one of us and we will burn forever."

"Mister Foresight is burning now," The Maitresse added. "Our friend and protector, Henri is burning as we speak and he will burn forever."

"Then there is no need for another of us to join him. Not yet," Maxine added. "Not until we know for sure."

"A Son of Light," Mister Monoxide said with the mild irritation of a man repeating himself, "must be reported to the Secretary."

Maxine answered with more force than expected. "But we don't know what has happened. We don't know it was a Son of Light. You're just guessing and you can't be certain. Maybe it was something else. Maybe it was something that we don't understand. Maybe the One True Lord couldn't protect him for reasons we cannot comprehend. You don't know."

The Maitresse Bathory raised her hand to quiet her. "The Hands is right about uncertainty," she said, "We don't know what happened to Henri. But we should make all efforts to discover and remove doubt. Then, and only then, should we consider summoning the Secretary. But we should be under no illusion. If there is a Son of Light, he..."

"…He'll hunt us and kill us," The Pain interrupted. "And if he knew who Henri was then he may know who we all are."

"Then we gather more information," Mister Monoxide said. "Sentinel, we'll need you to speak with the police. Use your privilege. Examine their investigation and gather as much information as you can."

"And if their evidence suggests it's a Son of Light?"

"Then we summon the Secretary. We tell her what we have found. And then we bare witness as she kills one of us."

CHAPTER FOUR

Doctor Luke Edwards' chin lowered to his chest as he read the name of Nikki Bannister. Sometimes patients acted against their own self-interests. This should have been yesterday's problem but he couldn't reach the doctor requesting the call.

"Come on, Luke," he whispered. "We've not lost yet." He dialled the number. "Good morning, I'm trying to reach Doctor Christodoulou. My name is Luke Edwards, I'm calling from..."

"…Yes, Doctor Edwards, I am Christodoulou, thank you for getting in touch. I have one of your service users who was brought in as a suicide attempt. Nicola Bannister."

Luke tried to sit in a power posture, with his head high and shoulders back, yet he couldn't quite stop himself from shrinking a little into the chair. "Yes. I was asked to give you a call. How can I help?"

"We're looking to pass her to mental health services but the closest open place is outside of London. I spoke with Doctor Hill yesterday and he suggested, as you have a good rapport with her, she could be passed to you as an outpatient."

"Yes. I think that's perhaps the best idea. She has

a long running health management programme organised through her GP. I'll email her doctor first and if everybody is in agreement I'll make the arrangements to start daily inpatient care."

----- X -----

As Charles Peachtree got closer to Highgate he began to sense the dark aura that emanated from this part of London. The rolling hills of the area stood atop dark forces. Muswell Hill, Highgate Hill, Crouch Hill, they were all capstones to a great and terrible force that Charles could attune himself to.

"Mister Peachtree, hello." The priest, Paul Benjamin, was almost running to see him. "How good of you to come, Sir. It's always an honour." Peachtree smelled of fat-man sebum, layered with aftershaves. Despite the foul stench, the priest stood closer than was comfortable.

Charles handed over a supermarket plastic bag. "The Maitresse sent you this. Clean it and keep the bones."

"Certainly, Sir. Right away."

"Please tell me the fucking elevator is working."

Father Benjamin cradled the wrapped plastic bag as though it was a child. "Yes, Mister Peachtree, it's working. Would you like to visit the temple?"

Without answering, Charles walked to the back of the church and into a vestry with the priest in tow.

Behind a curtain, part of the floor had been excavated to reveal a temporary elevator, the sort used during the construction of high rise apartments, where the motor unit was at ground level rather than above. Charles Peachtree was so large he barely made it into the cage. "I'll send it back up for you. Follow me down."

The ride took almost a minute, descending first through a crypt, then into what looked like a brick-walled well. The Victorian engineers who dug this shaft had sealed and cemented the walls with fine workmanship and quality materials. Attached to the wall was an iron ladder for times when the elevator failed.

At the bottom, the lights were already on. Four sets of powerful lamps stood on tripods, all pointing to the glossy black floor. A pentagram, twelve feet wide was etched in white. Charles Peachtree began his slow walk of the pentagram whilst behind him the elevator began its ascent.

He could feel it. He could sense the power from this place. There were twelve possible locations The Prince could be reborn, but every time Charles visited this place it felt more likely to be this one.

Behind him, the elevator began its descent and he heard the cage door open as it arrived. "Is everything to your satisfaction, Sir?"

Charles held his hands out, his palms facing the centre of the pentagram like a man warming by a fire. "It feels good," he whispered. "It feels okay. We've had a setback and I wanted to make sure I can still feel the One

True Lord."

"Have I done a good job, Sir? Keeping the place ready?"

Charles turned his fat bulk towards the elevator and shuffled to the cage without answering. The priest kept himself tight behind, intruding into his personal body space. "Do you want something?" he growled.

"I was wondering, Sir... I was…" the priest was flustered. He took a deep breath and made his question. "Sir. Would you like me to suck your cock again?"

"No."

----- X -----

Mister Deathmask watched as the fat man left the church. Charles Peachtree called himself The Pain and Mister Deathmask hated him despite having never met in person. When Peachtree got into his car, the suspension took the hit of the obesity and the whole car seemed to sag on one side. The fat man was disgusting. "I'll see you tonight," he whispered.

He turned his attention back to the church. Why would a servant of The Disease come here? Was the church important?

Mister Deathmask entered the building. It was a simple, traditional chapel, perhaps large enough for two hundred worshippers.

"Can I help you?" the priest came to him quickly. "We're not open. The hours of worship are posted outside."

"I want to pray."

"You can come back for evening mass at seven if you wish."

"I want to pray, now."

The priest held one hand ahead of Mister Deathmask and guided his attention towards the door. Mister Deathmask leaned closer to the man and took in his ethereal scent. This was no man of God. He was a servant. The lowest kind of servant. The worthless and disposable kind. "You have to go," the priest reiterated.

Mister Deathmask stared at the priest for a moment then walked backwards in little steps towards the door, keeping the holy man in his sight. The priest was aligned with darkness. "I may come back for you," Mister Deathmask said.

"Yes, come back at seven."

As he left Mister Deathmask whispered, "I'm doing something else at seven."

----- X -----

Charles Peachtree took off his shit stained pants and hung them over the back of the armchair. He preferred to be nude. He lifted a huge bowl to his lap that contained the entire contents of a multipack bag of crisps, twelve packs in one. Being this gelatinous required a dedicated diet. It was all part of his blessing. He enjoyed being lazy and the blessing of the One True Lord meant he could live however he wanted without caring what others thought.

He pressed a button on the remote control and the old VHS video player whirred into life. Seen naked, his belly hung so low between his legs that his belly-button covered his penis and the hanging flab rolled over the edge of the chair between his knees. Above his navel was his pentagram.

Maxine Elsworth and The Maitresse were on the video. A home-movie from almost twenty years ago. The younger Maxine held the back of a teenage boy's neck. "Why the fuck did you come here, you little faggot?"

The kid was coughing and spluttering as he tried to take his clothes off. Charles snorted a laugh at the screen and scratched his balls. "Don't upset The Hands," he said.

Whilst the kid on screen undressed, The Maitresse sat in a chair snipping a pair of scissors together. "Do you have a girlfriend? Because I'm going to turn you into a woman."

The Hands forced the boy to lay flat on his back. "Shall I take the camera?" The picture wobbled and shot the ceiling as it was passed between them. The younger Charles Peachtree appeared, already stripped except for colourful Hawaiian shorts.

Watching his home movie, Charles scratched his ass, ate some crisps, then pushed his hand under the roll of flab to roll his cock-end between thumb and forefinger. It was the closest he could get to masturbating.

On the screen, his younger self lay on top of the boy, who began to scream with an untold agony. The Hands used her gift to shut the boy up as The Pain unleashed his namesake and began torturing the boy with skin to skin contact.

Skin upon skin, the fat-man versus his victim. Shock waves of electrical energy rushed through the nerves sending unimaginable torture across the nervous system of the boy. Burning, fierce, scorching, blistering pain. Maxine had once asked to try it. He'd rested the tip of his little finger against the tip of hers and let the pain run as gently as possible for only a second. She needed to lay down for an hour. She said it was agony uncontrolled.

There was a noise elsewhere in the house.

"What the hell?"

Glass broke. It sounded like it came from the kitchen.

"Is someone there?" Charles heaved his massive, naked bulk from the chair as the door opened. A man came in. A huge man wearing a long black coat, a bowler hat, and some kind of devil mask.

For a moment, Charles stared blankly, not even sure what he was looking at. The intruder rushed forward with raised fists. Gloved hands with brass knuckles. He threw his first punch and Charles felt his body counter with a speed no fat man should be able to reach and felt the pentagram on his stomach burn as the One True

Lord reached out from hell to protect him. A second punch came that was ducked just as easily and Charles countered by grabbing the man's coat and jamming his free hand under the devil mask, knocking off the hat. He had him, he had his bare hand pressed against his attacker's face and electrified the nerves of his fingers.

The attacker swung another punch, the brass knuckles practically splitting his left ear in half; but The Pain held fast and pressed his hand harder, getting a thumb into the man's mouth, pressing his fingers into the attacker's eyeballs and unleashing his gift with every ounce of his being. Another brass-knuckle punch came, this time to his right, then another to the left that grazed his head and practically tore his eyebrow off.

Pain… Unleash the pain… unleash the pain…

It wasn't working.

Oh, Fuck!

"Help me!" He stumbled backwards as a barrage of blows began tearing the skin from his face. "My Lord." There was an explosion in his right eye as he was blinded in a blow that also sliced back the skin to a loose flap around his cheek. "MY LORD!" Another hit to the jaw and he felt his face deform as the bone cracked. "MY LORD?" A massive uppercut smashed his teeth together causing him to bite off the tip of his tongue. "Why have you forsaken me?"

This shouldn't happen.

This couldn't happen.

Oh, Fuck!

Charles fell back, raising his hands to shield his face and as he went to ground the punches stopped. Through his blurred left eye, he watched as the Son of Light paused to straighten his devil mask and collect his bowler hat. "You mother fucker." His voice slurred and blood poured from his mouth as dark slime. "You fucking black cunt," he slurred. "You fucking nigger!"

The attacker ignored the race-bait and brought out a folding knife. The man straddled him and began flaying the pentagram from his stomach. "NO! NEVER! NEVER!" Charles screamed and began fighting back with renewed vigour. He was suddenly imbued with the strength of ten men to fight his way out through desperation. He kicked whilst lying on his back, blood flying up the walls from the slice to his belly. He got a bloody leg up between him and the Son of Light who now stabbed at his foot and ankle. He kicked the man back with just enough space to allow him to roll over and kneel. His flabby paunch hung low, the skin with the pentagram was peeled off, but it wasn't taken yet. This fucker couldn't have the mark. The One True Lord had touched him with his own hand. He'd physically blessed him. No Son of Light would ever take his pentagram. Bloodied and blinded, Charles clung to the hanging slice of flesh, holding it against his belly. "You won't take this," he slurred. More blood poured from his mouth and ran between his flabby man-breasts. "You won't take this."

From behind there was a low 'whoosh' sound.

Ignition.

As he looked back over his shoulder a blast of fire came from the Son of Light as burning petrol sprayed across his back.

He had no strength left, no gift, no hope, but as his body was sprayed with burning fuel he kept hold of his pentagram; at least he would keep that.

----- X -----

Mister Deathmask opened the French doors overlooking the garden and allowed the smoke to escape. Charles Peachtree had collapsed under his own weight and his blackened corpse smelled of burned pork.

A video played on the television. A young man sat naked in an armchair whilst an old woman with bloody hands knelt between his legs. The boy looked serene, as though he'd been tortured so much he had no more screams to give. Mister Deathmask turned his attention back to Charles Peachtree.

He heaved and strained to roll the dead man onto his back, but once in position he got to work with his waxed paper, placing the scroll over the fat-man's face. The wax liquefying as the backing burned, running into the gashes and gouges of a smashed face. Another wonderful trophy for Magdalena. He rested it by the door to cool and sat on the edge of the armchair. The video had changed. The castration porn had ended and the tape had run into another episode of filth. On screen was a young girl of perhaps twelve or thirteen years old wearing a light blue dress. She was in a walk-in closet. Women's shoes were all around and the young girl was being commanded to lick the soles of them, cleaning them with her tongue whilst an older woman barked orders at her.

Mister Deathmask felt a swell of emotion. "Innocent," he whispered. "She is innocent."

Somebody else spoke in the video. "We're going to make you clean more than shoes with that pretty mouth."

Mister Deathmask punched the TV screen so hard his fist went through the glass. A few sparks popped around his wrist and he wore the flat panel TV like a bangle. He yanked his hand back throwing the shattered TV screen across the room.

Bastards.

These people were vile.

They were protected and believed they could do anything.

But he would stop them.

He had to stop them.

----- X -----

Grace Chelimo was a visual cliché. With her pinstriped business suit and size six waistline, she looked like she'd stepped from a stock photo of 'successful black woman.' She sipped her cappuccino and slid the brown envelope across the table. "For your troubles," she said.

The detective quickly put it in her handbag.

"There's another murder," she said. "We think it's linked."

"Linked to Henri Bonheur?"

"Yes. In fact, it's probably the same killer, which is going to escalate things."

Grace took another sip of her coffee. "What happened?"

"There was an unusual waxy residue on Monsieur Bonheur's face. The forensic lab sent it for specialised testing. Then this morning we heard back from the laboratory saying a near identical case came in. Like Bonheur, the body was beaten and burned, but what caught the laboratory's attention is the second murdered man had the same waxy residue on his face."

Grace sat more attentively. "Do you know who was murdered?"

"Yes, his name was Charles Peachtree."

----- X -----

Beneath Almassy House, Grace Chelimo had worked herself into a state of agitation. "I can't believe it," she repeated near endlessly. "Nobody can physically touch The Pain. It should be impossible."

The Maitresse Bathory asked, "How is our anonymity? What do the police know of us?"

"Nothing. They know nothing other than Mister Foresight and The Pain were killed in the same way and probably by the same person."

"That person seems to know who we are," Maxine said. "I can't believe he took The Pain. It's inconceivable. He touched me once. Nobody can touch The Pain. Nobody."

"Nobody could sneak up on Mister Foresight either, but it happened." Mister Monoxide took a deep inhalation of his life-ending gasses. "First Henri, now Charles. We must summon her. There is no question on what we are facing."

"One of us has to die," Maxine said. "One of us will burn in hell forever."

"Henri and Charles are already burning," Mister Monoxide added. "There is no other option. We know the law and we know what is happening. There is a Son of Light hunting us and we must summon The Secretary."

Merry Murder spoke quietly, "When?"

"As soon as is practical," Monoxide said. "We are permitted one day to prepare, so tomorrow evening would be suitable."

"I'm not ready to die," Maxine whispered loud enough to be heard.

Mister Monoxide took another big inhalation through the medical mask. "None of us are. But the One True Lord has written the law that we follow. We may award ourselves one day to prepare. Drink and eat well. Satisfy your pleasures and enjoy your day on Earth as though it is your last. Then we will summon The Secretary and her bidding will be our pleasure."

CHAPTER FIVE

"Good morning, Luke." The reception nurse handed him a clipboard of appointments. "Doctor Hill called to say he has a family emergency and won't be here today or tomorrow. I've shuffled the appointments around but there are two high-concern service users added to the list."

"Okay, thank you." He looked at the list. Nikki Bannister was on there. He flicked through the notes looking for the suicide attempt. "Abney Park," he said aloud. It was the cemetery. Her previous suicide attempt was in the same place. Then there was a new note on her file that made him freeze. Nikki Bannister was recently infected with HIV. "Now there's a complication."

"Homerton Hospital has referred you back to us and I see that you've had an injury. I last saw you three months ago and you were doing well, so, can you tell me what led up to hurting yourself?"

Nikki Bannister looked like a wasted rock chick. Eighteen years old with greasy black hair to her shoulders and a crude playing card tattoo behind her left ear. The ace of spades. "I'm sorry to be a burden," she murmured. Already tears were welling in her eyes.

"You're not a burden," Luke replied. He passed the box of tissues to her and spoke softly and warmly. "I know we've talked before about how our brain is an organ, like our lungs or kidneys, an organ can be fit and healthy or it can have illnesses. If your lungs are unwell you'll find it hard to breathe and if your brain is unwell it can make you feel unhappy, but that doesn't make you a burden."

"But it's all gone to shit this time." She blurted her words with a sob that blew a snot bubble from her nostril. "Everything has gone to shit."

"Tell me what has happened. When did you first get the feeling to harm yourself?"

"When I knew I had AIDS."

"Your G.P. messaged to say you were recently diagnosed with HIV. Can you tell me how that came about?"

Nikki shook her head. "It's not my fault. I knew straight away. It wasn't my fault."

"What wasn't your fault?"

She took a moment to compose herself, three deep breaths. "I went to a party and met a man. A Russian. He must have put something in my drink; this wasn't my fault. Please, believe me when I say that." She looked up and made solid eye contact. "This wasn't my fault."

"What happened?"

Her head drooped low again. "I woke up the next

day at a hotel. He'd had sex with me and, I don't know what he'd done but I was hurt… you know… between my legs was very sore and I was bleeding." She took a few more deep breaths and steeled her nerves. "He'd written on me with lipstick. It said AIDS."

Luke closed his eyes and rested a finger against his temple. "Okay. Do you know this man, do you know how to find him?"

"I think he said his name was Vich, or Vlad. I don't remember because I was so sick and forgetful afterwards. I was trying to get home and couldn't keep my eyes open. I was exhausted. I was tired for days."

"Is there anything you remember about him?"

"Scorpions. He had tattoos of scorpions all over his back and on his neck."

Luke jotted it down. Scorpion tattoos were common in the gay community as a sign of HIV infection.

The girl cried a little harder and held her hand up as a gesture not to ask anything. She needed a moment to get it out. "It wasn't my fault," she sobbed.

"When did this happen?"

"A few weeks ago. I was doing okay. I was doing everything you taught me. I was making time to make myself happy. I was following the exercises. I was eating at the right times and going to bed at the right times." She dipped her head low again and dabbed the tissue at her eyes. "I was following the rules. I was doing everything right."

"What makes you think you were drugged. What were the symptoms?"

"I was tired and unable to control what was happening. I remember being in a taxi with him and couldn't think properly. It's the one thing I am sure about. I'm sure I was drugged."

"And then there was a gap before you hurt yourself?"

She sobbed. "I don't want to live anymore. I want to be with my brother." She suddenly burst out with a massive wail. "I want to be with Calum. I want to be with my brother and my Mum. I want us to be together again. When I die we can be together. We can be happy. We can be a family." She turned her hand over to look at her bandaged wrist and cried.

----- X -----

Merry Murder parked his car outside the hospital and stared at the asses of two staff-nurses. Their uniforms were unflattering. Dark blue trousers with pale blue tops. Back in the olden-days nurses were sexy, now they were made to look as frumpy as possible. That wouldn't stop his imaginations on what he could do to them. "Later," he mumbled to himself.

In his office he unlocked his desk drawer to retrieve a flash stick of computer files. Photographs. The ones he liked to look at when nobody was around. He put it into the computer and browsed the images. The office girl was first, he'd strangled her with her own stockings. Then came the wayward teenager he'd suspended from an exposed beam in a derelict factory; he'd drowned her by resting her head in a bucket of dirty water. The next photo was taken on holiday in Florida. He'd tied weight-lifting dumbbells to a precocious thirteen-year-old's feet with her father's silk ties and tossed her in the swimming pool. The next image was one of his favourites; a woman bank clerk who was rude to him. She was tied to a chair still wearing her banking uniform, he'd ripped her uniform to get her tits out and a clear plastic bag over her head had slowly suffocated her. Such joy. This was what elevated himself above normal people. The One True Lord had blessed him and opened a world of consequence free perversion and eternal life. His desire to hurt women had frustrated him to the point of madness; that was when the One True Lord had offered him the chance to do as he wished, free of consequence. How could he refuse? All those frustrations and urges could be satisfied. It seemed the deal of a lifetime.

Tomorrow, that deal of a lifetime could become the horror of eternity.

"A fucking Son of Light," he mumbled. "All of this misery, from a fucking Son of Light."

He left the office with his flash stick of memories. If the Secretary chose him, somebody would go through his possessions and find these images. He wasn't ashamed for his crimes to become public after he died, but this was personal. He'd spent quality time toying with these women. The time he'd spent killing them were his memories. His. They were not for the enjoyment of normal people. They weren't for sharing.

Luke Edwards passed in the corridor. "Oh, Doctor Hill, I didn't know you were here today."

"I just came to pick something up. I won't be in tomorrow either."

Behind them Nikki shuffled out of the consulting room and took a seat in the waiting area. Merry Murder felt a swelling in his groin but played innocent, pretending not to remember her. "Who is that girl?"

"Nikki Banister. We talked about her. Her baby brother was killed in the park, he was snatched and…"

"…the kid was murdered. Yes, I remember. She attempted suicide." Merry Murder couldn't take his eyes off her. Such victimhood. Best of all, she was suicidal.

"Things took a bad turn. She was drugged and raped."

Merry Murder had to shield his mouth with a hand to maintain the pretence of being shocked without betraying a smile. "Oh, no."

"That's not even the worst of it. Its resulted in her being infected with HIV."

The doctor opened his mouth to speak, but just left it hanging open. It was too perfect. Life had tortured this young girl with a cruelty of extraordinary scale. "That's terrible." He said it with a flutter of excitement.

"I assessed her and she needs inpatient care. I was

about to try St. Ann's. I don't hold much hope of getting a space without sectioning but… I don't know… She's lucid and cognizant, but she is definitely high risk."

"Let me call St. Ann's for you. A few people there owe me favours."

"You don't mind?"

The good doctor tapped Luke on the arm. "Leave it with me."

He went back to his office and waited a moment for Luke to clear the corridor, then he crossed the floor to the medications room and took a bottle of Droperidol and a hypodermic syringe. The Droperidol was used as a chemical restraint. One quick shot and that poor girl would be immobile and unthinking. He could already imagine giving it to her. He could jab her in the buttock and squeeze the confusing liquid into her tight little ass. He didn't need to inject her to take her, the power of his voice was enough to seduce a woman, but he enjoyed his hypodermic fetish. It was a great joy of male doctors to inject drugs into women. It was penetration.

He returned to his office and pretended to make a phone call whilst toying with the loaded hypodermic. He kept watch through a crack in the door. The girl was in view. She had her elbows on her knees and her head hanging low. Her hair looked greasy. She looked defeated. "I'll cure you of your suicide fetish," he whispered. "I'll have you begging to stay alive."

Luke Edwards appeared in the corridor again as Merry Murder stepped out. "Good news, Luke. I think we have something for Miss Bannister. I'm heading over to St. Ann's and can take her in my car if you could introduce us."

Luke led the way. "Nikki?" Slowly her head raised to make eye contact. "Nikki, this is Doctor Hill."

Merry Murder smiled and said, "Hello, Nikki."

"He can admit you as an inpatient at St. Ann's and would like to take you there."

Nikki half nodded. "Okay. You mean right now? Shall I come with you?"

Merry Murder fought back his smile. The young helpless girl was asking for permission to leave with him. "Yes," he said. "Come with me now."

----- X -----

The doctor walked her to the carpark. He had a strange manner to him; up front he seemed like a warm caring person, but Nikki sensed a coldness underneath. It was as though his words were kind but his eyes were cruel. There was something not right about him. "How are you feeling, Nikki?" he asked. "Your emotions? Are you stressed or anxious?"

"I'm feeling overwhelmed by everything." She fidgeted and played with her hair.

"Don't worry, we'll change that." He motioned towards a silver Mercedes. "This is my car." He pressed a button on the key fob to unlock the doors. "Come and get in."

Nikki did as she was told.

Merry Murder got into the driver's seat beside her and spoke in words that drifted and soothed. "I want you to relaaaaaax, Nikkiiiii."

She softened. The words were as smooth as silk. "Did you say something?" she asked.

"Yessss, Nikkiiiii," the words came as a hiss. "Ressst back in the chaaaaair." As the words hit, she felt her muscles go weak and her eyes become fixed. "Rest a moment, Nikkiiii." He held up a syringe. "I'm going to injeeeect youuuu wiiith thissss."

"Why?" her response was docile. Sleepy.

"For myyyyyy pleasuuuure."

He pulled off the protective cap to expose the needle.

"Why?" she whispered. Her words came slowly. They seemed to echo. "Why?" the echo lingered. "Why?"

"Just relaaaax, Nikkiiii. Feel yourself sleeeeeeep."

She felt a sting in her leg that snapped her out of the dream state. The doctor had his fist against her leg.

Wrong. He was touching her or…

"Relaaaxxxxx," he hissed. For a moment the dreamlike state returned, but the sting to her leg kept the hypnosis at bay. She opened the door and pulled back. She got one leg out and yanked her second leg away from under the doctor's grasp. She was out of the car within seconds but whatever he'd done caused her leg to give way the moment she stepped on it. She fell on her ass and slumped forward to lean against the side of the car.

Something was wrong. She couldn't move. She couldn't think. She was going light-headed like she was about to pass-out, but the unconsciousness didn't come. She managed to slur a single word. "What?"

Echoing footsteps came around the car. She could feel herself being lifted. "There, now," the doctor was saying. "I think you fell out of the car." He was lifting her up. Pushing her back in. He was lifting her feet and putting them into the car one at a time. He was fastening the seatbelt across her, placing the strap between her breasts and spending more time adjusting her breasts than the belt.

There was a voice in Nikki's head, her own voice. It asked her a question. "Do you want to go to sleep?" She didn't have to think about it for long. "Yes."

Then she was asleep and everything had gone grey.

----- X -----

Nikki's eyes opened and she found herself shivering and damp. Her eyes didn't seem to focus properly. It was an effort. She was groggy. She couldn't see properly. With effort, she rolled to her side and hit a wall. There was a mild smell of chlorine like a swimming pool.

She was naked.

As she moved there was a clinking of metal and something moved against her hand that startled her. "Whaaa… Where am I?" God, she just wanted to sleep… No. Wait… she was naked in the dark.

Instinctively, she pulled her arms across her chest. "Oh, fuck. Oh, fuck, where am I?"

She fell back against the wall, hearing the clinking of a chain as she moved. It was dark except for a dim spot of light above. Just enough light to show her surroundings and… oh, God… there was a chain around her waist. The links were small, maybe an inch, there was a loop around her waist and padlocked tight across her navel.

"Jesus… fucking hell… HELP!"

Nikki began coiling in the chain, pulling the loose links in and found the end. She expected the other end to be fixed onto something but instead it just hung free. "Help," she called out again, "Help me, hel…" she stopped short. Who had put her here? Where was she? She was with the doctor. He whispered something to her that made her sleepy. He stabbed her leg with something.

Nikki's heart was pounding so hard and her breathing so rapid in fight or flight mode that the cold was forgotten. Her eyes adjusted. She was in a cell of some kind. Perhaps six feet wide and about seven feet high, maybe a little higher. "Get out of here," she whispered to herself. "I've got to get out of here." She felt the grogginess come back as she tried to stand, a feeling of drunkenness, a bad hangover where the world spun when she turned her head. She felt her way along the contours of the room and discovered a sealed door with rounded edges, like a ship bulkhead. Was she in a ship? The floor was wet and in the centre of the floor was a drain.

"Oh, shit… Oh, shit… Oh, fuck…"

The panic rose fast.

She felt further around the cell, the chain around her waist hung between her legs and she stepped on it as she tried to manoeuvre, toppling her forward. One wall was reflective, she could see herself naked in the dark reflection.

The doctor… Oh, fuck… he did something to her in the car and now she was in some kind of cell. Was it the hospital? Had they put her in a special cell at the hospital?

Suddenly panic hit her like an explosion and she hammered her fists against the door, the metal reverberating with each hit. "Help. Help me… Please. Anybody. Help me… HELP! HELP!" Her fists bashed against the door. Jesus Christ. Jesus fucking Christ. She was locked in a tiny damp cell. Stripped naked and chained up. "HELP!" She screamed. She cried. She wailed. "HELP ME. PLEASE. JESUS CHRIST, HELP ME!"

----- X -----

Merry Murder was frying a fine fillet steak and had already opened the bottle of Chateau Petrus. The wine cost thousands per bottle but as it could be his last day on Earth he would indulge. Of course, money didn't matter so long as Jason Kinnear kept bringing them their millions. Mister Market was certainly useful, especially when it came to their living standards, but tomorrow night one of them would be chosen by The Secretary. Whoever she chose would die and suffer a fate worse than death, pain beyond compare in perpetuity.

The good doctor spoke to himself as he cooked. "There are only six of us left," he mused. "Henri and Charles are gone, so who will she choose?"

Who was expendable? The Hands was probably the most powerful, Maxine Elsworth could put her grip on anybody and bend them to her will, she was the enforcer. Mister Market brought them the finances for the mission. It was hard to imagine The Secretary taking either of them. Nor would she take Sentinel; Grace Chelimo was protected beyond all. No, The Secretary would never choose her. That only left the Maitresse Bathory, Mister Monoxide and himself. The Maitresse had her uses, she could track anybody better than a bloodhound and had the right attitude for the work whilst Mister Monoxide was the brains of their little group.

Merry Murder rolled the wine around his tongue. "It won't be me," he said, but it could be and he knew it. In fact, it was likely to be him. He was the weakest member of The Circle. The Secretary would kill him and ride his soul back to hell. "Fuck this realm," he whispered. "Fuck them all."

He finished cooking his steak and served it with petit pois, fine beans and baby broccoli. He enjoyed it as much as any death row convict enjoyed their final meal.

There was a one in six chance he would die tomorrow.

More likely it was one in three.

Likely, it was him.

In his study, he rested his wine glass and the remaining half bottle on the pedestal table. The room was panelled in dark wood. The pedestal desk was vintage walnut. The reading chair was burgundy leather. Along one wall was a fitted bookcase filled with everything from classics to the modern tomes of pseudo-intellectuals. He wasn't a great reader but he enjoyed having a bookshelf that made him look like one.

"To the One True Lord," he said raising his glass. "May you bless me and keep me safe. May you acknowledge my devotion to you."

Merry Murder ran his finger across the spines of the books. Behind one was the small brass hook that worked as a handle. The bookcase rolled back on castors, swinging towards him as a door. He put a vinyl record on the deck and fine jazz began to play. Behind his chair was a compact video camera, he started recording as the soothing music filled the room. When all was ready he took his seat in the reading chair and enjoyed the view.

There was a naked girl behind the bookcase, trapped in a glass fronted cell.

Her eyes were wide and she was cowered against the back wall, holding one hand across her breasts and another across her pubis. It was cute, her bottom was stuck out behind her as she tried to cower. "Please," she begged. "Please let me go."

Magnificent.

The girl was already begging. This one had given nothing to the world. Suicide attempts for attention, then HIV from being a filthy, fuck-machine. Merry Murder took the remote control, and pressed the button that closed the drain, then pressed another button that brightened the spotlight above the girl's head and the dark rust-coloured walls of her cell. Finally, he pressed the button to turn on the powerful shower heads and water deluged onto the girl.

She shrieked.

She shivered.

Her hands tried to shield her as the ice-water hammered down with the force of a fire hose. Then her hands went to the bulkhead door and tried to press against it. She turned around in the cell, covering herself again as she came to face front.

The water was up to her ankles and rising; and that was when it happened. That wonderful moment when the penny drops. The moment of victimhood. She recognised and understood. The water wasn't draining away.

Merry Murder leaned back in his chair with a glass of Chateau Petrus. His entertainment for tonight would be the beautiful agony of a trapped girl, panicking as she drowned.

----- X -----

The shower hit like a pressure hose and the streams stung like needles. "Stop!" Nikki was yelling. "What are you doing?" She leaned against the bulkhead door and hit her fist against it, the bandage around her wrist, that she'd kept dry on medical advice was now soaking wet. The water was quickly above her knees.

The glass. Try to break the glass.

She hammered her fists against it. The doctor was sitting in a chair sipping red wine with a grin on his face. With his free hand, he gently waved through the air as though conducting a soft piece of music.

Think. She had to think.

The glass was thick, maybe a few inches, the sort used in a giant aquarium. She needed a hammer or something to get through it. She coiled the loose chain around her fist and punched in an action that hurt her hand more than the glass.

The water was rising to the top of her legs.

She looked up and shielded the spotlight with her hand. The top of the cell was smooth. There were no handholds that she could see. The shower heads were flat metal plates against the ceiling. It wasn't as if she could float up and grab onto something.

The chain… oh, God… now it made sense. It was to weigh her down. Sure, she could try to swim higher, but the chain around her waist would weigh her down.

Nikki hammered on the glass. "Please… Mister…

please I'll do whatever you want. You can fuck me. I'll be your sex bitch. I'll do anything you want." Then something broke in her spirit. Her head rocked back and her eyes closed and her body let out a terrified scream. Oh, God, she was going to drown.

Not drowning.

Please. Not drowning.

The water was to her breasts.

Nikki pressed against the glass with her hands open, palms against the glass. "Please, Mister… Please, don't do this… I'm sorry. I'll do whatever you want."

The water was to her armpits and she was beginning to feel buoyant.

The water passed her shoulders and was up to her chin. She moved back from the glass and looked down to the coil of chain by her feet. In her mind she felt a strange and sudden calm as though searching for the correct strategy. What was she supposed to do? Which part of the puzzle hadn't she fathomed? What was the trick to surviving this?

The water reached her mouth and she began jumping, letting the buoyancy lift her to take a breath. With each jump she got a breath, but with each descent she realised the water was getting deeper. She tried jamming her feet against the walls but there wasn't enough purchase and her soles slipped. Then she jumped from the bottom but her nose and mouth didn't fully clear the surface and she took in a mouthful of water. At first she panicked and flailed, fighting against the weight of the chain to break the surface but a survival instinct kicked in and a single thought went through her head that said, 'if you panic, you'll die.' It was enough to make her take stock, she allowed the chain to bring her down under the water and rested her feet on the floor, then kicked off the bottom, purging all the way up until she broke the surface and snatched a breath. She sculled for a few seconds, fighting against the weight of the chain then allowed the weight to pull her down ready to allow another hard kick off the bottom.

The strategy worked, but she knew it could only be temporary. How long can you keep trying to grasp breaths when you're chained in a cell that is filling with water?

Not long.

She kicked hard and broke the surface, the shower heads had stopped pouring. There was perhaps a foot of breathing space from the top of the water to the ceiling, there really was nothing to hang on to. The cell had been designed that way. Designed. Jesus, fucking Christ, somebody had designed this thing.

She submerged, planted her feet and kicked off again, snatching a breath and treading water before the weight of the chain pulled her back down. Adrenaline was keeping her going but her muscles were already screaming out for relief. On the next kick she barely made a mouthful of air.

As she touched down she considered not even trying. What was the point? But the rational thought of death wasn't as strong as the autonomic need to breathe. She kicked off the bottom and swam hard to try and take another snatch of oxygen.

Then she sank lower and paused to look at the doctor. Even through the water and glass she could see him sitting in his chair with his glass of wine and… the door was opening behind him. Somebody was coming into the room. Somebody else.

She kicked off and fought, somehow finding a new dose of strength knowing there was somebody else to plead with, but again she barely got more than a mouthful of air.

There was noise. A thump against the glass as the doctor slammed against it. There was a man in the room with him. The doctor crashed against the glass, his back against the cell as a man threw punch after punch. Then the doctor was pulled forward and spun around. He crashed against the glass again. This time his face hit and it left an explosion of blood.

Nikki tried to jump but stepped on the chain and lost her momentum. In panic, she tried to claw her way to the surface and burned through all the air in her lungs as she flailed. This time she really panicked and took water into her nose and mouth. She tried to recompose and sank again but this time saw a crazy devil in a bowler hat looking into the cell. Blood was streaked down the outside of the glass and the room was on fire. There was a man with the face of a red devil looking into her drowning cell. She saw the doctor running away. In a final roll of the dice she screamed the word, "HELP!" to the devil man, releasing a stream of bubbles from her mouth.

She tried for the surface one more time.

She failed.

She sank and tried to position her feet for another jump to the surface but her body was going weak and she suddenly lost her orientation, not knowing which way was up or down.

Outside, the devil man began punching at the glass with what looked like hammers on his hands; trying to break into the cell.

It was going dark.

The room was on fire. Was she going to hell?

Then beside Nikki appeared a ghostly little girl, her white dress flowing in the water. She had no eyes but her hands reached out and touched Nikki's face, then she floated away, seemingly passing through the bulkhead door like a ghost.

The devil man stopped punching. The ghost girl was outside in the burning room. Her hand was pointing to something.

It was the last thing Nikki Bannister saw.

CHAPTER SIX

The girl lost consciousness. The chain held her midway to the surface.

Mister Deathmask punched his brass knuckles into the glass. Magdalena appeared. "Behind the books."

There was a 'whoof' sound as something flammable in the desk ignited. Magdalena vanished. Deathmask shook the bookcase. It was attached to the wall on one edge. The fire rushed up the curtains and flames licked out across the ceiling as the room filled with smoke.

Behind the books?

He swept his arm behind a row of hardbacks and threw them to the floor. There was a small brass lever. He pulled it and the unit unlocked and swung out, but then stuck against the books on the floor. A sudden billowing of black smoke filled the room. He couldn't breathe. He yanked the furniture back to find a small anteroom that that held a pocket of clean air. A light shone onto a bulkhead door. His hands were on it, throwing the clamps from each corner. A trickle of water pouring from the bottom as he spun the wheel, feeling it loosen, seeing water pour from the edges; then it burst and pushed back as several cubic metres of water flushed a naked girl into his lap.

"Please," he yelled. "Please, lady. Wake up!"

The girl was lifeless. The water rushed out of the anteroom and into the study extinguishing the carpet fire. The space filled with smoke to near blackout. He fought to push the girl aside and stand. The smoke stung his eyes and the heat was blistering. He hooked one hand under the girl to drag her.

The fire was up the walls and bookcases, the flames across the ceiling sucked air from the room and the carpet gave off a steam of toxic chemicals.

As he dragged her, the girl spasmed in his grip. Her head fell limply and her mouth frothed with a foaming mousse. He pulled her through the passageway and dragged her to the front door.

The doctor was sitting in his car beyond the garden. He had the engine running.

Deathmask dropped the girl and ran but only managed five paces before the car was at full speed. Red tail lights vanished into the distance.

Smoke rose above the house to the incessant beeping of smoke alarms. The girl coughed and rolled. She tried to sit up. He crouched by her side and helped her onto all fours whilst she sucked in deep breaths between sobs. "I save you," he said. "This man tried to kill you, but I save you."

The girl's face was white, her eyes were wide and she was cowering away, visibly shaking. It was the mask.

Mister Deathmask took off his hat and mask, then

he took off his coat and placed it over her shoulders. He wanted to cover her nudity, he wanted to prove his gentleness. "He tried to kill you," he said. "I won't let him."

----- X -----

The devil man led Nikki with an arm across her shoulders. He led her to a dark blue car. What the hell was happening? He opened the door and tossed his hat and mask inside. The man looked like a vagrant. He was black, with the face of an ex-boxer, a man with chipped teeth and thick lips. "Please," he said. "We must get away."

Thick smoke was drifting into the street. "Who are you?" she asked.

"I am an angel."

He was crazy.

Nikki backed away. She turned and started jogging barefoot, the chain coiled up in one hand whilst the other clutched the coat lapels together. She needed the police. She needed help and although part of her instinctively wanted to scream out and yell to raise the alarm, she was too frightened of antagonising the big man. She heard him follow. She turned to face him, "Please let me go."

"Magdalena said to save you. I must protect you."

"Who is Magdalena?"

"Did you see her? She was in the water with you."

Had that been real? Was there a ghost with her in

97

the water? "What does she look like, Magdalena?"

"She is beautiful. A little girl with white skin and long dark hair. You saw her in the water with you."

Nikki felt a whoosh of emotion. Fear and wonder, terror and amazement all meshed together. "I saw a ghost."

"She asked me to save you." Then he said something that sent a shiver along her spine. "She will come back to speak with you soon."

Behind them, a man taking his dog for an evening walk noticed smoke blowing into the street. He was looking at the house and making the phone call. "Hello? I need the fire brigade."

"Please. We must leave. I will protect you until Magdalena returns."

The smoke blew into Nikki's eyes. Soon there would be sirens and fire fighters.

There had been a ghost in the water with her.

"We must go," he said again. "The doctor who try to drown you has friends. Magdalena found you. We must go before the doctor or his friends come."

"He is coming back?" she gasped. "No… I don't want to… I need to get away." She couldn't focus on what her choices were. She was biting her lip. Turning around and looking at the street for some clue as to what she should do. "I don't know."

"Please, you must come with me. The doctor will return with his friends. I will protect you but we must go."

They drove away, passing a fire engine coming in the other direction with blue flashing lights and siren wailing.

----- X -----

They stopped at a row of lockup garages. "We hide this car and walk, now," Deathmask said. Nikki hobbled on the uneven surface by the garages. She lifted one foot to brush away a small sharp stone as her rescuer locked the garage door. Nikki watched him, noticing the brass canister hung from his shoulder. He wore a dark brown shirt and baggy trousers that looked almost worn through.

"Why were you there?" Nikki asked. "Why were you at the doctor's house?"

"He is a bad man and I came to stop him hurting people."

Nikki swallowed hard. "Were you watching him? Do you know what he did to me?"

The big man lowered his head and spoke softly, he looked like a man trying to show subservience. "He is called Merry Murder. He kills women and girls for enjoyment. Magdalena sent me to stop him."

"Magdalena? What is she, really?"

"You will see soon. She is coming to speak with you. She will explain." He ushered the way, then stopped, looking down to Nikki's bare feet. "Please. Wait." He took off his shoes by standing on the heel of one and pulling his foot out. They were worn brogues, badly scuffed with the heels worn down. He knelt to offer them like a servant before a queen.

"I don't need them."

"Please."

"No. I'm fine. Really."

He said it again, but with an air of desperation, lowering his body even closer to the ground. "Please. Please take them." He rested the shoes ahead of Nikki. They looked huge against her feet.

"I think they're too big."

"It is only to walk to my home. It will be better. Please."

With a sigh, Nikki stepped into the shoes that were like boats on her little feet.

They walked for fifteen minutes to the derelict home. The front hedgerow was so overgrown Nikki had to push it aside with her forearm to get through the gate. The building itself had broken windows held in place with wooden boards. The paintwork was peeled and the garden grass was almost a foot high.

Deathmask led the way to the rear and into the kitchen. There was a smell of stale sweat.

Nikki stepped out of the shoes but continued to grip the overcoat around her. "Do you have any clothes?"

"I can give you the clothes I am wearing now if you are cold. I can buy you clothes tomorrow." He pulled the chair from the kitchen table for her.

"You said Magdalena is coming?"

"Yes. Soon."

"How soon?"

Deathmask shrugged. "In perhaps a few hours, perhaps even in the morning. She will come when she is strong again. I can feel her. She wishes to speak with you very much."

----- X -----

Merry Murder was driving too fast without a destination. "Calm down, Peter," he whispered to himself. "It's okay, you're away." He pulled in by the side of the road. His hands were shaking and his whole body was jacked on adrenaline and fear. "Oh, fuck… oh, fuck… oh, fuck…" He punched the steering wheel, "FUUUUUCK!" He turned on the courtesy light to see blood flecked across his hands and on the upholstery. His face hurt like it had been hit with a hammer a dozen times.

What in unholy fuck was that thing?

He needed help.

The professor would know what to do.

----- X -----

Mister Monoxide was in his private cinema watching a grainy black and white film of a Nazi death camp. On the screen, a naked Jewish man fell into a pit alongside a hundred corpses. He held a flame to the glass pipe, heating the Zyklon B pellets whilst inhaling; the gas-chamber chemistry wasn't the mellow high that carbon monoxide was, but it was authentic to the movie. In his days at medical school he'd fallen under the spell of opiates and worried his addiction would kill him. That was when the One True Lord offered all the poisons of the world without fear of the consequences. On screen, a firing squad lined up prisoners. "Kill those fucking Jew cunts," he whispered.

The telephone rang.

"Good evening, Peter. How are you enjoying your…"

"...The Son of Light just attacked me."

"WHAT? Wait a moment." It took a few seconds to clear the Zyklon B from his system and focus his mind. "Okay, I'm ready. Tell me what happened."

"I was at home. This big, black, motherfucker came in and started knocking six types of shit out of me."

"Where is he now?"

Merry Murder's words became garbled.

"Peter?" Mister Monoxide pressed the phone against his ear. "Peter, are you still there?"

"Yeah, I'm here," he gasped. "I had a girl to enjoy. The Son of Light came for me, but took an interest in the girl and I was able to escape. He is fucking strong. I mean really fucking strong. It was like fighting a bull. I nearly fucking died."

"Okay. I'm going to call the others and let them know what has happened. Come to my place. We'll meet up and move out. If this thing knows where we live we need to move to safety. I'll ask Sentinel to protect us."

----- X -----

The comedown from the shock and terror was giving way to fatigue; Nikki's mind was alert, but her body was exhausted. The big man stayed in the kitchen with her. "Who are you?" she asked.

"I am Magdalena's angel."

"But what do I call you? What is your name?"

The big man shrugged. "I don't have a real name."

"Everybody has a name."

"I have a special name, but I have forgotten my real name. It was meaningless. I was chosen by Magdalena to be her angel and I am merely here to do her bidding, a vessel to be used for her needs, not my own. I have no life but to serve Magdalena. She chose me."

"You have no life?" Nikki screwed her face. "I don't understand what you mean."

"My life is only to serve Magdalena. My life is hers." He looked up to the ceiling and held his hand out as a signal for silence. Nikki's eyes followed his. For a moment the atmosphere felt electrified. "She is here," he said. "Magdalena is upstairs." He jumped from the chair and ushered Nikki. "Quickly. She can only stay a few minutes."

He led the way, his feet banging hard on the bare

wooden stairs. Nikki walked more carefully, the chain around her waist coiled in her hand.

On the landing, she saw a doorway to a room begin to glow with candlelight. The big man was in the doorway with his back to her, mumbling words to somebody inside. He came out with a grin and beckoned Nikki forward. "Remember, she is here only a few minutes."

Nikki edged in, craning her neck to see inside the room without committing. There was a girl with long dark hair standing in the corner. She wore a white dress and faced away, her back to Nikki.

"What is your name?" the girl asked. Nikki jumped as the door was closed behind her. There were faces on the walls. Plaster casts of broken and damaged faces. "Your name?" the girl asked again.

"Nikki… are you Magdalena?"

"Yes."

"I saw you in the water." Nikki swallowed hard. "I thought I imagined it. I thought you had no eyes."

The girl remained with her back to Nikki. "I have no eyes," she whispered. "They were cut from me when I was alive. My eyes were a blessing for this." Her hand pointed to a dresser on which was an ornate knife. The handle was engraved whalebone, the blade silver, the top of the handle embellished with a large red gemstone in a silver bezel. "Many years ago, a woman cut my eyes out with this knife as a gift to The Disease. She entombed me in a cellar, she blinded me, then fixed me in a cell with stone and mortar until I died of starvation; and I want my revenge."

Nikki glanced around the room; the casts of broken faces were horrifying. "Why do you want to speak with me?"

Her voice was whispery, "Because our future lay together. I can see into your soul. I can see your pain. You wanted to die. Only when a man tried to take your life did you find the will to live, but a time will come when those thoughts of death will rise again. When that happens, when you wish to die, I have something to offer in place of death."

Nikki's voice came without volume, a mere gasp of air. "What?"

"Together we can make a Handshake of Light, an agreement to become one and the same. A being of the light."

Nikki shook her head. The girl was ungodly, freakish. "I just want to go."

"There are people in this world who will hold you down. Their own lives are built upon your suffering. But there is another way. You can reject them and join me in handshake. We will become something unique. We can punish those who hurt the innocent. It is the fulfilment you seek."

"And how does this happen?"

Magdalena's hand raised to point at the knife. "Kill yourself with this."

"What?"

"With this knife, kill yourself so that the tip of the

blade is within your heart when it stops beating."

Nikki stepped back towards the door, her hand feeling behind her for the handle. "No."

"You wanted to die," Magdalena said. "You wanted to die so much. This way, you live again with me. Die by this knife and we can become one. Together we can punish those who hurt innocence."

Nikki turned the handle and opened the door. The big man was blocking her exit.

"Look at me, Nikki," Magdalena said.

"I'm frightened."

"Let me reveal a truth."

Nikki turned back and watched as the little girl raised onto her tiptoes, her bare feet barely touching the floorboards. Then she lifted higher, rising into the air until her feet floated two feet from the ground.

"My God." Nikki clasped her hands over her mouth and felt the hands of the big man rest upon her shoulders, standing behind her, holding her steady.

Magdalena drifted sideways and her tiny child hand reached for the knife on the dresser. "Let me show you what Leonora did to me." With her hair floating freely around her head, Magdalena rotated and drifted towards Nikki.

"Oh, fuck!" Nikki gasped. "What the fuck? What the fuck?" She backed up the last few inches until she was pressed against the man behind her.

The little girl had dark holes in her face where her eyes should be. Below the wound were black streaks showing where the blood had run. They looked like stains. Tattoo markings of where she'd bled from her eye sockets.

The floating Magdalena held the knife ahead of her and drifted towards Nikki. "Leonora cut out my eyes with this knife. It is a very powerful thing and it can be the source of our salvation. Kill yourself with this knife and we can be together. We can be strong. Make the Handshake of Light and become one with me." The ghost came closer and handed the knife to Deathmask. As the knife was passed, Magdalena's form took on transparency, the candlelight flickering through her body. "Be with me," she whispered. "Together, you and I." Her head tilted upwards towards the man. "Tell her everything. Protect her."

Magdalena vanished.

----- X -----

The home was a beautiful townhouse with a crescent driveway and pillars by the front door. Mister Monoxide was standing on the porch, waiting, the small gas cylinder in one hand and the breathing mask pressed to his face in the other. Merry Murder's car skidded to a halt. "He's a big, black, monster of a cunt. Over six feet tall and he has the strength of a tank."

Mister Monoxide slowly pressed his hand down as though pumping a brake. "Take a moment to compose yourself, Peter."

"He nearly fucking killed me," Merry Murder gasped.

"How badly are you injured?"

"I don't know? My face hurts like fuck. How do I look?"

"Like an injury lawyer's wet dream." Mister Monoxide stepped back and ushered him inside, gesturing towards a mirror in the hallway. Merry Murder gasped when he saw himself. There was blood soaked into his clothing from a wide gash in his brow. He looked like he'd been sliced open, but the wound was more of a dent in the swollen lump of his forehead. His face was covered in bloody streaks.

"He hit me," the doctor said whilst tentatively touching the wounds. "He had like, I don't know, some kind of metal on his fists and fire came out of his hand. I know that sounds weird, but he held his hand out like this," he demonstrated reaching out, "and fire shot out from the palm of his hand. He set my fucking house on fire."

"You escaped. The Pain and Mister Foresight didn't."

Merry Murder used the washroom in the lobby, running water into his cupped hands to rinse his face. He left the door open to speak. "He is a Son of Light. There's no doubt about it... He was... I don't know how to explain, just a feeling really, but he was protected in some way. He was too strong. Too powerful." He rubbed tentatively at the wounds. "I should be dead. There is no way to fight him physically, not one-on-one. The only reason I got away is he was distracted by my plaything."

"Where was the last place you saw him?"

"At my home. I came straight here. Fuck. I had a video camera running that may have filmed him, but it's probably burnt to shit now."

Mister Monoxide pressed his surgical breathing mask over his face, breathing in and out slowly for three breaths. "I will call Sentinel and have her take weapons to Almassy House. I think we should go there. The Son of Light knew where you lived, as he did with The Pain and Mister Foresight. Staying in our homes isn't wise."

Merry Murder nodded, then stated the obvious, "We need to call The Secretary." As he said it his voice went high with a wave of emotion. He'd survived an attack from the Son of Light, but he wouldn't survive The Secretary.

----- X -----

Grace Chelimo was dreaming of hunting a man. She was in a jungle, carrying a bolt-action rifle with a telescopic scope. In her dream she caught sight of a shirtless black man with scars across his back. She was about to shoot when a voice in her head whispered, "Alive." The word was so powerful it was like an earthquake running through her bones. It was the One True Lord.

She sat up in bed and let the covers fall away. It was a message. She was about to get a phone call. The message came from…

…her telephone rang. The display read Prof. Richard Tudor.

"Mister Monoxide. I've just been contacted."

"Sentinel, are you alright? Are you safe?"

"Safe? Yes, I'm safe. I've just been awakened by the One True Lord. He awakened me with a dream."

"When?"

"Moments before you called. Literally seconds."

"Sentinel, we have a problem. The Son of Light attacked Merry Murder, he is injured but will survive. The Son of Light was at his home less than twenty minutes ago which means he could be close to you." As he spoke, Sentinel got out of bed, her white silk sheets fell away to reveal her athletic physique. "I believe the Son of Light knows where we all are and I want to bring everybody to Almassy House. I want you to bring weapons to defend us."

Sentinel began running down the stairs of her home, not stopping for a robe. "I think that was my message," she said. "It was one word. It said 'Alive' but it came in a dream moments before I was to kill a man." At the ground floor she opened another doorway and ran to her basement, hitting the light switch as she went.

"We're going to summon The Secretary. But I want you to bring weapons to protect The Circle. If the Son of Light knows where we live then you are our only defence."

"I understand," Sentinel said. "I'll be there as soon

as I can." She ended the call.

She scanned the basement as the fluorescent lights revealed her personal gun range.

Along one wall were revolvers and automatic pistols of varying makes and models. The first she took was her go-to weapon of choice, the Volquartsen Scorpion, the most accurate semi-automatic pistol in the world. Hers was matt black, customised by slimming it down to reduce weight and extending the barrel with a compensator to increase the accuracy even further. As a target pistol it didn't have much stopping power but when matched with her gift of deadshot it was unbeatable. Body armour was no defence against a woman who, in a split second, could shoot through your carotid artery at a hundred yards.

She scanned the room. Light SMG's were best for urban defence. Heckler and Koch MP7 was the choice, especially if she ended up shooting in the catacombs of Almassy House. Tight, twisting corridors meant there wasn't the manoeuvring space for a long weapon… But then again, the One True Lord had said, 'Alive.' Was she supposed to capture this man?

She had two X26 taser pistols; they were worth taking.

She began loading up.

The One True Lord had contacted her directly. She was still loved. She was still useful. She was still chosen. That was when she realised she was crying tears of joy. Her original mission had been a failure. It wasn't her fault, but although the One True Lord hadn't punished her for that failure, she carried the guilt of it every day. But now, the One True Lord had a purpose for her. She wouldn't fail this time. She would never fail again.

----- X -----

The first light was filtering through the window of the trophy room. Nikki was curled on the mattress with the coat clutched around her. Her exposed feet were as cold as ice but she hadn't any way to cover them or the courage to ask for a blanket. She believed the big man had stayed in the kitchen overnight. She'd remained simply because she wasn't sure what else she could do. It was like a nightmare. A bad dream of murderous doctors and ghostly little girls. Things were terrifying. But amongst the strangeness the big man offered an indescribable tranquillity; being with him was somehow better than being outside and alone. He had rescued her. He had covered her nudity. He had offered his own shoes. He had promised to tell her everything. He had made a sworn promise to protect her. Until she had clothes and the chain unfastened from her waist, she would go along with what he wanted.

There was a knock on the door. "Are you awake? May I come in?"

Nikki sat up on the mattress. "Yes."

He came in with two plastic bags of clothes and a bolt cutter. "Please. We can try this." He opened the cutter handles as wide as they would go, a motion that opened the blades by barely an inch. Nikki opened the coat. "Here," he pointed at the padlock. He positioned the blades against the steel hoop and Nikki held it true as he closed the long handles and snipped the metal like it was pasta.

The chain uncoiled and fell over her hips. "Thank you," she whispered.

"I have clothes for you. Different sizes." He upended the bags and out tumbled thrift-shop dresses and shoes. He'd bought a selection of fashions that Nikki would never normally wear. She liked black jeans and T-shirts. The big man had brought her flowered dresses and worn trainers.

"I need privacy," she said.

"I will make coffee whilst you dress. Then I will tell you everything. Like Magdalena said. I will tell you everything."

----- X -----

From the bag of thrift store clothing, Nikki chose a short sleeved, dark blue dress with small white polka-dots and a grey cardigan. She sat with Deathmask in the kitchen. "It began with a Swedish man called Iohann Axel," he began. "He was very evil and he worshiped the devil. This is many hundreds of years ago. He is the one who made this." Deathmask rested the ornamental knife on the table. "There are twelve of these. Made from twelve

113

innocent children."

"Magdalena is one of the children?"

"Yes. The children are called the Twelve of Darkness, and this knife is the Eye of Magdalena. From the twelve children, nine of them are light; Magdalena, Mary, Jesus, Sebastian, Kaifus, Rasmus, Peter, Brecht, and Jansen." He took a deep breath and showed some anxiety. "Then there are three who have made a dark handshake. Elijah, Pontius and Jacob."

"Magdalena said something about making a handshake."

"A Handshake of Light. Magdalena wants to become one with you."

Nikki put her face in her hands. The whole thing was too bizarre. "I don't understand any of what you are telling me."

The big man rested his palms on the table either side of the knife. "Many years ago, the Swedish man, took the twelve children to a Church of Satan in the Carpathian Mountains, what you now call Romania. He took the children into a chamber deep below the church. Using these knives, a woman called Leonora Goral blinded the children to bless the knives in glory to the devil. Leonora Goral became Secretary to Satan."

Nikki shook her head. "You mean actual Satan? The devil?"

"Yes."

"I don't believe in the devil. I don't believe in God and I don't…"

"...it is true. You have met Magdalena. You saw her. You spoke with her."

She took a breath. "I don't know what she is."

"The Secretary cut out Magdalena's eyes with this knife." He slid the knife closer to Nikki but she didn't touch it. "The Secretary entombed Magdalena in a cell in the Church of Satan. The children were blinded and entombed until they died of hunger. Now I help Magdalena find The Secretary so that Magdalena can take her revenge. She will become one with you and together, in a Handshake of Light you can protect the innocent."

"Magdalena wants me to kill myself."

"Yes. You kill yourself with this knife. If the blade is in your heart when it stops beating you will become an angel with Magdalena."

"But I don't want to kill myself." She said it firmly but her breath gave out as the realisation sunk in. Her right hand moved to cover the wound to her left wrist. The slice was undressed, held together with sutures that looked like the legs of dead flies. "I don't want this. I just want to be alone."

Deathmask took the knife off the table and put it back inside his coat. He spoke softer, taking his time with his words. "Do you know the man who tried to kill you last night?"

Nikki shook her head. "He is a doctor at the depression clinic. That's all I know."

"He is called Merry Murder. He kills women for enjoyment. He has friends like him. His friends are

Mister Monoxide, Mister Market, Sentinel, the Maitresse Bathory and The Hands. Together they form a circle devoted to the worship of Satan. But they are not just worshippers. They are blessed by Satan. They have been touched and branded by him, gifted, in exchange for carrying out a mission on his behalf."

"What mission?"

"To prepare the way for his son."

Nikki looked at him directly. "The son of the devil?" She smiled a little, just the gesture, there was no happiness behind it. "You're making this sound like a horror film."

"He was here once, the son. He died. He was stopped by another like me. A man we called Lice. He killed the devil's son, right here in London."

"When was this?"

"A few years ago. He was foolish, the son. He was filled with arrogance and hubris. He was a foolish boy. Of course he was protected by many and he was protected by the woman who calls herself Sentinel. She was his bodyguard; but Lice was cunning and he destroyed the son. It is through the work of Lice that I found the woman called Sentinel and through Sentinel I found the doctor who had you last night." The big man smiled widely and a tear, perhaps from joy, rolled from one eye. "Now that Lice is gone, I have taken his place. I am a Son of Light, as was he. I will protect the innocent, as did he. I will prevent them in their mission and I will help Magdalena take her revenge on The Secretary."

Nikki leaned back in the chair. "I'm not sure if you're insane, or I am?"

"You are not insane, nor am I. You have been brought into a world that few can see. You are entering the light, but there are agents of darkness that swirl about us. People like Merry Murder. People like Sentinel."

"Merry Murder? That's a crazy sounding name."

"It is their special name."

"Do you have a special name?"

"Yes, I have a special name. I am Mister Deathmask."

CHAPTER SEVEN

There were twenty, plastic white sacks of charcoal in the ground floor office of Almassy Partners. Mister Monoxide looked resigned. "We need to take all of these downstairs."

"Manual labour?" The Maitresse asked.

"I couldn't allow the deliverers to carry them down." He picked one up and demonstrated that it wasn't heavy. "They're quite lightweight, just unwieldy. It will take us a few journeys."

The Maitresse pursed her lips and furrowed her brow. "Very well. If there's no other option." She dragged her bag rather than lifting it, she moved like a sulking child. The Hands dragged a bag in similar fashion.

Mister Market lifted one bag, put it under his arm, then lifted a second. "I think us chaps can carry two at a time."

Mister Monoxide and Merry Murder copied his two bag style.

Sentinel followed them down with the two tasers in her hands. She would protect the rear rather than carry charcoal. If the Son of Light showed, she would deal with him.

The bags were dumped in the cave and Sentinel

began back up the stairs. Merry Murder lost his momentum and leaned against the wall.

"You're not out of breath already are you?" Mister Monoxide rested a hand on his friend's shoulder. "What is it?"

"I'm building my own gallows."

"It is just as easily my gallows. But we must accept death with pride and courage. We must face our demise with the conviction we have lived well; and we have lived so very well, my friend." He pressed Merry Murder away from the wall and walked him to the stairs, keeping a hand on his shoulder.

They moved the bags of charcoal down over the course of an hour. On their last trip, Merry Murder opened the door from the office and stared towards the lobby.

"You're not thinking of running, are you?"

"No. I just wanted to see daylight. I wanted to see the sun one last time." Merry Murder closed the office door, collected the final bags and started down. He wondered whether he would ever feel the sun on his skin again? Would he taste another fine wine? Would he ever laugh again? When you come to the end you start to realise how many things you've already done for the last time. A recognition that your last kiss has already happened, your last act of making love, your last morning of waking up.

"Bring the bags here," Mister Monoxide instructed. At the far end of the cavern was a raised lip of brickwork signifying a circle almost fifteen feet in diameter. He split open the first sack and began spreading the coals, inviting the others to copy. To one side was a long chest from which he pulled a gardening rake and used it to spread out the briquettes. He worked hard, losing himself to the manual labour, getting into the zone of honest toil. It was better to do that than dwell on what was going to happen

----- X -----

"Does anybody want to do anything, or say anything first?" Mister Monoxide already had a box of firelighters at the ready. He was tearing open the foil packets and spilling out what looked like small bars of soap.

It was the Maitresse Bathory who cut the silence. "We're as ready as we'll ever be, Professor."

Mister Monoxide began lighting the firelighters and stuffing them under the charcoal, walking backwards across the pit. He laid out fifteen of them then went back to the trunk for a bottle of accelerant. "Stand back." He sprayed the fuel which blew up in swirls of flames. The heat hit like opening the door to an oven.

The coals began to whiten with ash, then darken with glowing edges. Flames licked up in places. Above them, the smoke and odours vented away through a natural chimney. The cavern roof ascended to a point, then broke into a crack that went all the way to the outside; but although the smoke would rise, the heat was trapped in the cave and within minutes it was unbearably hot.

"Make the circle," the Maitresse said.

The Hands turned off the lights and Sentinel left her post to join them. The embers glowed red to illuminate the congregation, their faces shimmering through rising heat.

"Ave Satana," the Maitresse called.

"Ave Satana," they replied in unison.

"Hail, to the One True Lord."

In chorus they called, "Hail, to the One True Lord."

"God of our flesh, God of our minds, God of our will. We offer our praise that you may send us your guidance. We offer our lives that we may hear your wisdom and pledge our eternal suffering that we may be given an audience. Ave Satana."

The group called, "Ave Satana."

With a proud voice, Mister Market yelled, "Hail He who invites us to become as gods."

"Ave Satana."

"Hail He, who is the bearer of true Light," The Hands said.

"Ave Satana."

"Hail He who…" Merry Murder began his exaltation but lost his voice. Oh, fuck… was this how it happened? Was your voice taken first?

"Hail He, whose power is without question," Mister Monoxide called in place of his friend.

"Ave Satana."

All eyes returned to Merry Murder. He took a deep breath and bellowed his salutation. "Hail He, for whom I would suffer eternal anguish." As he spoke the rocks of the fire pit sturred and the air in the room began to pull closer as though a breeze were at their backs. A vibration was felt through the floor and the stirring in the centre of the pit became more frenzied.

"Oh, mighty Lord," The Hands called out. It was as though she was about to recite another self-abasing platitude but had forgotten half way. She hadn't forgotten, she just didn't need to say it.

In the pit, the coals were moving as though something underneath was pressing upwards. It moved in waves, swirling around, throwing sparks and flames high from the disturbance. The heat suddenly blasted upon them and the moisture on their brows ran across their faces, their clothes moistened as their bodies sweat, whilst in the pit the coals broke apart as a dark shape rose through the burning charcoal.

The shape opened its eyes.

"Praise be to the One True Lord," Mister Market yelled.

The figure raised higher, a head and shoulders visible. It was a woman, born from the fire. Her hair was thick and dark, her features that of a Roma Gypsy. Through her nose was a gold ring with a chain that looped to her ear. Her body rose higher still to reveal her as naked. Her skin was dark, her breasts swollen, her nipples pierced with hoops of gold. In her navel was a golden broach, her fingers were adorned with golden rings and her wrists with golden bangles. As her hips and ass emerged it revealed a burning pubis, the thick black hair of her cunt was alight with purple flames that licked across her stomach.

"Praise be to the One True Lord," Mister Market yelled again. "Praise be. Praise be."

Merry Murder found himself mesmerised and terrified in equal measure. The Secretary would kill him to return to hell. But looking at her beauty, her curves and dusky skin, she was as exotically beautiful as she was deadly. "Hail be to Satan," he said in barely more than a whisper. "Hail to my One True Lord."

With her final reveal, The Secretary stepped above the burning coals with feet that kicked up flames with each step. Around her ankles were golden hoops and her toes were adorned with golden rings. The Secretary arched, leaning back to raise her breasts high and let her head droop behind her. With gentle shakes of her head, the burning embers dropped from her hair. In the hairline was a fine golden chain that carried a pendant that hung on her forehead.

Slowly she returned her posture upright. She walked past Mister Monoxide, looking into his eyes. She stepped to the Maitresse Bathory and stared at her with equal measure curiosity and barely disguised contempt. With every step, more flames came from the coals, licking up her legs. She stepped past Mister Market and

The Hands, then Merry Murder. At the end of her walk around the pit was Sentinel and she held out a hand as though she would touch her cheek. In a growling voice she spoke the name, "Sentinel."

A tear rolled across Sentinel's cheek. "You can take me," she whispered. "I failed and I am prepared to suffer."

The Secretary lowered her hand. She didn't respond to the offer but the look of contempt she had shown the others softened to pathos when it came to the lawyer. Her gaze remained on Sentinel for a moment then she returned to the centre of the fire and rested her hands on her hips. "Why?"

"We have discovered a Son of Light," Mister Monoxide said. "In the past days we have lost two of our members to him. We almost lost a third."

The Secretary took a step towards him. The flames from her burning pubis grew more intense and followed the contours of her abdomen, curving around her breasts. "Your Lord knows this. But I do not see your Son of Light here."

"We respectfully called for you, as is our duty. We discovered a Son of…"

"…And your Lord guided you," The Secretary interrupted. "Your Lord communicated to Sentinel. She relayed his message to you." She looked back over her shoulder, "You told them your Lord wanted you to take the Son of Light alive, did you not?"

Sentinel looked down. "Yes."

"Poor Sentinel. Yet again you are failed by those who surround you." The Secretary walked the edge of the pit. "The Lord has a new mission for you. The opportunity to resolve your debt has changed. Capture the Son of Light, bring him here and summon me, then I shall take his soul. With this act the debt you owe to your Lord will be cleared and you may live eternally."

With each person she passed, she stared deeply into their eyes as though weighing up the value of their souls. When she passed Sentinel again the lawyer said, "Please. Take me."

"Your past and future are special, Sentinel. Do as I ask, then when it is your turn we shall make love in the fire together."

With a screeching wail, a flurry of sparks shot into the air and coals were thrown out of the pit as the Secretary flew across the circle faster than a trapdoor spider. Her hands grabbed Mister Market. "They don't need money to capture a Son of Light." With unfathomable strength, she lifted him in an arc over her head to drop him flat on his back in the centre of the fire. For a second, Mister Market looked as though he didn't feel the heat, but then the screaming came as his clothes began to burn. He rolled to his front and tried to stand and run, but all it did was sink his feet down to his knees in burning embers.

The Secretary kicked him in his face, knocking him onto his back, his feet still deeply buried. She jumped forward to straddle him as though about to fuck. Mister

Market screamed and swung his arms, one of his fingers caught in the golden hoop through The Secretary's right breast. She took hold of his wrists and held him down, pressing his arms into the coals. "Scream now for your failure," she said. "Scream for eternity under my torture."

For a brief moment, Merry Murder made eye-contact with Mister Market. 'I'm glad it's you and not me,' he thought.

The Secretary began to sink into the coals, pushing Mister Market lower. He screamed in unconscionable pain as his hair caught fire. The Secretary pressed him deeper. Her final words were growled directly. "I'm going to make you my bitch."

A second later they were gone.

The fire changed, closing the portal it had been, but even so, for a minute none of them moved. It was The Hands who broke the silence. "Maitresse... Can you find a Son of Light?"

Weakly, she replied, "I don't know."

"He is looking for us," Mister Monoxide said. "If we wait long enough, he will deliver himself."

Merry Murder coughed to clear his throat and wiped his brow with his sleeve. "There's the girl I took. I was killing her when The Son of Light showed up. He rescued her. She may know something."

Mister Monoxide looked to the Maitresse. "You could find the girl, yes?"

"I should be able to find her and we can hurt her until she talks. I'll need something of hers, a photograph or an item of her clothing."

"I have a medical file," Merry Murder said. "I have her address, her name, everything."

The Maitresse Bathory nodded. "Then I can find her."

----- X -----

The Maitresse Bathory shielded her eyes with one hand whilst holding her hat with the other. After hours in the cavern, the daylight was overbearing. Mister Monoxide smiled at her. "We are so close, Maitresse. So close to earning our rightful place."

"Yes, but I have to find him first."

"I have her case file at the hospital," Merry Murder said.

"Peter, is there anything you can tell me about the Son of Light. Anything that might help me track him directly?"

The doctor shrugged his shoulders. "He's big, he's black, he's strong like a horse and he smells bad."

The Maitresse smirked. "That hardly narrows it down."

Mister Monoxide took a breath from his mask. "Sentinel, do you have what you need to capture this thing? When The Maitresse locates him, we'll be relying on you to physically capture him."

Sentinel shrugged. "I can shoot through his hands and feet to weaken him, but we'll need to restrain him.

Ropes, or handcuffs. Something to tie him up with."

"I have handcuffs," The Maitresse said. "I have manacles and heavy restraints at my home."

"Then we should collect those first, then go to the hospital for information on the girl. We'll stay together so that Sentinel is close to us all."

The cars were in a private basement parking lot a few doors away. Mister Monoxide had a vintage, Rolls Royce Silver Cloud in two-tones, caramel and chocolate; Sentinel drove a powerful, silver-grey BMW. Mister Monoxide gestured towards his car. "Maitresse, Hands, would you ride with me, please."

Sentinel got into her car and gestured for Merry Murder to get in with her. Once inside she reached out to touch his chin and gently turned his head, scrutinising his wounds. "You're lucky to have survived," she said.

"Do you mean from the Son of Light, or The Secretary?"

Sentinel dropped her gaze. "I wanted to be chosen. She could have had me over Jason."

"I don't think you mean that, not really."

"I do really. I lost The Lord's Son and I deserve to be punished... Tell me about the girl you had last night; was there something special about her?"

"No, nothing. She's a suicidal nobody. She was a patient at the clinic I chose at random. I had her in my drowning tank; I was listening to music and drinking wine when suddenly this mother fucker comes into the room and starts throwing me around. He knocked me about like a rag doll and smashed me off the walls. The only thing that saved me is he noticed the girl underwater and stopped to rescue her."

"What did he look like? His face?"

"He wore a mask. Kind of a devil mask. You know those things they wear in Japanese theatre. They have freaky looking masks, like samurai and laughing clowns and stuff?"

"Noh theatre. I wonder if that's significant?"

"How so?"

"Noh theatre normally tells the story of a supernatural being who becomes human."

"I think the Son of Light has powers like we do. He's really strong, he had the strength of a rhinoceros and I think that strength could be a gift."

Sentinel stared into space as she remembered the past. "When I lost The Lord's Son, that Son of Light was quiet, he was almost invisible. He could slip by unnoticed. He could vanish in a crowd or disappear into the shadows."

"You know what scares me the most? This guy killed Mister Foresight. Henri was the one person it should be impossible to murder; and then Charles, surely The Pain would have touched him. Maybe, this Son of Light's gift negates our own. Maybe he will be able to evade The Maitresse, or maybe you can't shoot straight when you aim at him?"

"If that happens then we all dive in and beat the son of a bitch with our bare hands." Sentinel started the engine. "Because one thing's for sure. If we don't find him, he'll find us."

----- X -----

Mister Monoxide stopped his car in the grounds of The Maitresse' country home. As The Maitresse headed inside she said, "You can wait here. I'll have my faggots do the heavy lifting."

Mister Monoxide leaned against his car and took a deep breath from his poison mask. Sentinel and Merry Murder pulled up behind them. "I think this is good fortune," he said to The Hands. "I'm excited for this new mission. It has a neatly defined end point. We deliver the Son of Light and our success is assured."

"I'm afraid for that reason. What if Marigold can't find him?"

"Then he'll come to us. Eventually, he'll visit us and we'll be ready."

By the front door, The Maitresse reappeared with two naked men carrying what looked like heavy pieces of steel pipe, the men wore only leather collars around their necks and metal chastity cages around their genitals. A third naked man emerged carrying chains and a metal bar with leather cuffs on either end. Mister Monoxide opened the boot to the Rolls. "What is that?" he pointed to the pipes.

"They connect end to end to make a seven-foot-long pole," The Maitresse pointed out a big steel hoop at the top. "This is where you fix the restraints. You fix a man's hands to this hoop at the top, then his ankles to the one at the bottom and he's going nowhere."

Mister Monoxide looked over the naked men. The metal chastity cages around their penises looked like little bird-cages. "I must say, you have some marvellous toys. Why isn't this one caged?"

"He doesn't need it because I transformed him into a eunuch with a pair of pliers and a hammer."

Mister Monoxide took a deep breath through his mask. "My Dear, your cruelty is a blessing upon this Earth."

"That's very kind of you to say. Thank you."

The naked men carefully rested the chains, restraints and poles in the boot. When complete, the Maitresse said, "Go back to the house, you cunts." As they turned it revealed fresh whip marks across their backs, buttocks and legs. "Crawl, don't walk." The men got onto all fours and began crawling across the sharp gravel, their little caged pricks dangling between their legs.

Sentinel was leaning against her car, watching the crawling men. "I've just thought of something. I think you should all be armed. In case something happens and I can't protect you, you should all have guns."

----- X -----

They were stood in Sentinel's armoury. Weapons of

various kinds adorned the walls looking like a combination between a museum and a showroom. Rifles and assault weapons were on one wall, shotguns stood in racks. "I'm going to give each of you a revolver. They will all use the same thirty-eight calibre, hollow-point ammunition, so the bullets I give you can be used in any gun. The guns are snub-nose, double action revolvers, which means all you have to do is pull the trigger. They're the best thing for an inexperienced user under pressure." As she spoke she collected two pistols from the shelves then opened a drawer to find two more.

"Don't forget we need to capture this man alive," Mister Monoxide said.

"Yes, but I'm the first and only line of attack. If I fall, you need to stop him." She rested the guns on the table. "They're all as good as each other, but I think this will suit The Maitresse. It has a thinner handle for smaller hands, it was designed for petite ladies and children."

The Maitresse smiled and looked at the shiny nickel pistol, "Guns designed for children?"

"It's American."

The Maitresse chuckled. "Of course it is."

Sentinel showed the basic operation. How to open the cylinder and load the bullets, the safety mechanism, how they could choose whether to cock the hammer first or just pull the trigger to shoot. Once readied she led them to the shooting range so they could test fire their weapons.

They took turns on the range, practicing for at least

an hour. When not shooting, Sentinel drilled them on reloading the weapons.

Before leaving, Merry Murder asked, "How does our shooting compare to yours?"

Sentinel pulled a coin from her pocket and flipped it downrange. A split-second later she whipped out the target pistol and let off a single round that hit the coin in mid-air and sent it to the far end of the range at incredible speed. "The one True Lord guides me," she said. "I never miss."

----- X -----

"Get us a plain white van." Sentinel dropped Merry Murder at the rental depot. They realised The Maitresse Bathory's wonderful bondage pole would be impractical when assembled. There was no way to put a seven-foot pole with a spiritual being tied to it in either car.

Merry Murder brought the new vehicle and they transferred the restraints to the back. "Are you sure you're comfortable leaving the Rolls parked on the street?"

Mister Monoxide took a breath of poison. "Not really. It's my pride and joy. But on the other hand, we are possibly only a few hours from glory. I'm sure it will be safe."

----- X -----

Mister Deathmask's eyes drooped a little, they were slightly yellowed with fine red veins. "I am going to sleep for a few hours."

Nikki said, "I'm going home."

"No, you must not go. I must protect you like Magdalena asks."

"I can't stay here. I have to go."

Mister Deathmask was making wide shakes of his head. "No."

"You say you will protect me, but you can't keep me like a pet." She stood up. "I'm going home."

Mister Deathmask didn't rise from his chair. "Please don't. I will do as you ask, but I cannot protect you if you don't allow me to help."

"I'm going home. I want a few hours to think about what has happened."

"Then I will come for you later. I will come in a few hours."

Nikki smiled slightly, he didn't know where she lived. "Okay," she whispered.

"Magdalena will bring me to you."

Oh, great…

Mister Deathmask shuffled to the stairs. Nikki remained in the kitchen for a few minutes then quietly slipped out.

She looked back at the house. The overgrown bushes obscured it from the street. She walked the suburb not entirely sure where she was. At a row of shops, she asked how to get to the nearest Underground

Station and discovered she was in Finchley. It wouldn't take too long to get home, but with each step came an emptiness that quickly consumed her. What was she going home to? For what reason? Last night a man tried to kill her and she'd been saved, but for what purpose? So she could kill herself a different way? One man wanted to drown her whilst a little girl wanted her to stab her own heart. But what did she want? What did Nikki Bannister want?

"I think I just want to die," she whispered. She pulled up the sleeve of the cardigan to look at her stitches. The flesh surrounding the sutures felt squishy and tender. Now that she was away from the drama, now she had escaped the drowning tank, the mysterious Mister Deathmask and the ghostly Magdalena, all she could think of was how much better it would be to not exist. She still had HIV, still had a lifetime of drugs to put in her system.

What was the point?

----- X -----

"Hello Luke, I didn't expect you to be here at this time?" Doctor Hill was smiling, but had an authoritarian tone to his voice. Luke Edwards was sat at his desk with pages of handwritten notes spread out.

"Paperwork. I'm leaving shortly." His voice trailed away as four people entered the lobby.

Doctor Hill followed Luke's gaze. "They're with

me. I'm just here to collect some things. Have a good evening, Luke."

Luke went back to his notes but watched the strange arrivals. There was a mean looking black woman in combat pants whose face was screwed like she'd just bit into a lemon, an older woman with a grey hat and thin dry lips, a younger woman who looked like she was grinding her teeth in anger and a craggy old man with penny-lensed glasses. That man took a medical breathing mask from his pocket and made a big inhalation whilst glaring back at him.

The woman with the grey hat said to Doctor Hill, "Get what we came for. Get it now." The man with the breathing mask kept his gaze fixed on Luke.

Luke pulled his notes together and watched as Doctor Hill collected a patient file. Medical records were digital, but notes were handwritten during sessions. Then he saw Hill pass the case file to the old lady. That was unusual. Really unusual. Patient files are confidential and these people were clearly not mental health professionals. Then he heard the old lady speak sharply, "Nicola Bannister. Is this her address? I want to go there next." She flipped through the case file. "This is enough. I'll find the bitch."

Luke grabbed his coat and walked towards Doctor Hill. "Is there anything I can help you with?"

Doctor Hill took the file from the old woman and held it beside his leg. "No, Luke, everything is fine, thank you." The doctor and the mystery guests stared at him.

"Are you leaving now?"

"Yes."

The doctor gave him a nod and a wave, "Have a good night."

The black woman stared intensely. Luke gave a thin smile but lowered his gaze. She had a holster on her waist, under the jacket. Holy fuck. She had a gun of some kind on her belt. He saw it for only a second. He moved a little faster now, getting along the corridor to the elevator. The man with the breathing mask stepped into the corridor to watch him. As the elevator doors closed he saw him taking another inhalation whilst staring back.

What the hell?

Who were these people? Why did Doctor Hill want Nikki Bannister's case file and why the hell did the black woman have a gun? Did she really? It was a fleeting glance, so, maybe it was something else. Maybe he imagined it? He took his phone and called St. Ann's hospital. "Hi, can you put me through to admissions please."

"Hello, admissions."

"Hi. My name is Doctor Luke Edwards, I'd like to check the status of one of my service users that was transferred to you yesterday. Her name is Nicola Bannister."

There was the sound of typing. "What was the name again?"

"Bannister, Nicola Bannister. My name is Doctor Luke Edwards, I'm with the Complex Depression Unit."

"I'm sorry, Doctor Edwards, I have no registration for a Nicola Bannister."

"Where there any book-outs yesterday evening? Was there bed space? Is it possible she was transferred to another unit? She was brought to you directly by Doctor Peter Hill of the CDU."

"I don't know what to tell you," the woman said. "I have no admittance of a Nicola Bannister. Did you say Doctor Peter Hill?"

"Yes."

"Okay, let me search by that name. No, I have no patient or doctor record."

Bad thoughts flashed through Luke's mind. If he had not seen a gun, or imagined seeing a gun he would march back upstairs and ask what was happening. But the gun changed things. No. Surely he was imagining it. But what had the old woman said? 'We'll find the bitch?' Find who? Nikki? She was supposed to be at St. Ann's, Doctor Hill had taken her personally; and now he was looking for her along with a woman carrying a gun.

Something was seriously out of place.

Luke got into his car and watched. The group emerged from the hospital and crossed to a white van and a BMW. He scrutinised the black woman especially to try and see a weapon but her jacket was fastened and there was nothing to see. "Okay," he whispered. "Let's see what the computer says." He headed back to the office. He started up the computer and typed her name. Nicola Bannister.

Discharged.

She was let go, not transferred. Yesterday he'd felt she needed inpatient care. She was suicidal. She was a danger to herself. "Oh, My God!" She was discharged right now. The date and time were in the last fifteen minutes. Doctor Hill must have updated the computer record before he left to make it look as though she was discharged rather than transferred.

What the hell? Was this a crime?

"Shit… oh, shit… what the hell do I do?"

He looked up her number on the screen and called it from his mobile. As the phone rang in his ear he recalled what the old woman had said, 'Is this her address? I want to go there next.'

He checked the computer record. She lived in Stoke Newington. He could go there.

"Hi, this is Nikki, leave me a message."

Check up on her. Just call in to see if she was there and make sure she was safe. He could alibi himself. Yes. Just a routine check. Say he'd called St. Ann's to check on her and when she wasn't there he wanted to make sure she was okay. Yes, he could do that. He would go to her home.

CHAPTER EIGHT

"It's this one," Mister Monoxide pointed to the door. The Stoke Newington home was in a row of Victorian terraces just off the high-street. Lots of old homes here had been converted into flats and bedsits. The home had six doorbells; all of them looked out of order. The Hands pressed each bell in sequence then hammered her fist against the door. It was opened by a bare-footed hipster kid with a beard and a can of lager in his hands. "Yeah?"

The Hands took hold of his wrist. "I want Nicola Bannister, where is she?"

"Is she the goth chick? We get mail for somebody called Nicola Bannister. Is she the goth chick?"

The Hands walked the boy into a tight hallway. There were three doors on this level, each door had a lock indicating bedsits; at the far end of the hallway was a kitchen. Mister Monoxide pushed past and checked it out. "Who lives in these rooms?"

"I live in this one," he gestured to the first.

"And who lives with you?"

"Nobody. There's a Spanish girl lives in the front and a Polish guy called Boz or Baz or something who lives here. I think, the girl you want is the goth girl. She lives on the top floor with the tall blonde."

Sentinel was flicking through a collection of unopened envelopes by the front door. "There is mail with her name on it."

The Hands pressed hipster boy into the kitchen. "Take a seat." Then to Mister Monoxide, "Professor, could you give him a taste of your medicine?" Mister Monoxide handed the plastic mask to the boy; he had to stand close as the tube that ran to the small cylinder of poison was only a few feet in length. The Hands kept her fingers wrapped around the boy's wrist. "Hold it over your mouth and breathe it in." The boy did as he was told, pressing it against his beard. "Take a nice deep breath." He breathed from the mask then pushed it away, gasping for air. The Hands took hold of the mask and gently held it back over his mouth and nose. He slumped a little on the chair, his eyes rolled in his head for a few seconds before his eyelids drooped closed.

"That's enough, my dear," Mister Monoxide said taking his mask back.

The boy slipped off the chair to the floor, laying on his side and groaning out as the poison did its work. The thing with carbon monoxide is it clings to the red blood cells just like oxygen, but then refuses to let go. It only takes a few breaths for the blood to become saturated with a worthless asphyxiating poison that deprives the brain of oxygen. The light-headedness is a blast until it becomes permanent brain damage. It doesn't take long.

Merry Murder was still at the doorstep with The Maitresse Bathory. "Do you sense anything?"

142

"No. I don't think she is here, but I can sense something. This is a place she frequents. We will find clues here."

"Upstairs?"

The Maitresse nodded and gestured to the staircase. The Hands led the way closely followed by Sentinel. On the second floor was a communal bathroom that smelled from a combination of damp, soap and mould. "It's above," The Maitresse said. "I can almost smell her." They went higher. On the top floor was a kitchenette beside two more bedsit doors. The kitchenette had a sink, microwave oven, toaster, rack of knives and a kettle. The sink was filled with dirty coffee mugs.

The Hands knocked on the first door. A girl poked her head around the jamb, TV noise came from inside. "Yeah?"

The Hands grabbed her wrist and marched her back into the room revealing her to have Rapunzel length blonde hair and wearing only a T-shirt and pink thong. There was a young man spread out on the bed, equally undressed wearing only white socks and a pair of satin, zebra print briefs. He jumped up yelling, "Who the fuck are you?" There was a moment of standoff as both he and The Hands sized one another up, then he muscled himself between his girl and the intruding woman. "Get the fuck off her, let her go."

The Hands let go of the tall girl and grabbed the man instead. The moment her fingers were on his wrist he became docile but now it was the girl who began shouting. "What are you doing, you can't come in here, you can't…"

"…Hello, Sweet Cunt!" Sentinel had the barrel of the Volquartsen pressed to the bridge of her nose. The gun brought quiet.

The Hands led zebra-pants to the bed and sat him on the edge. She motioned towards The Maitresse Bathory. "This lady has questions for you."

"Where do I find Nicola Bannister?"

"He doesn't know Nikki," the girl said.

"Where is she?"

"I don't know. She lives in the next room. But she isn't here."

It was too tight in the bedsit for all of them. Mister Monoxide and Merry Murder were standing in the doorframe. Merry Murder backed out and tried the door to Nikki's bedsit; the handle rattled but the door didn't move. He kicked it hard, breaking the lock and swinging the door open to a room of stale air. Clothes on the floor. A mess of makeup across the sets of drawers. Half burned candles. Merry Murder opened the drawers, unsure what he was looking for. He found a red jelly dildo amongst her underwear; trespassing is always a joy when you uncover shameful secrets. The Maitresse joined him. "Ah, yes. I can smell her. I can sense her."

"Any ideas?"

"She is close. Less than a mile, maybe even half a mile." The Maitresse pressed her fist to her chest. "Oooh.

144

She is anguished. My goodness, this girl suffers. I can feel her pain, it will lead us to her."

Merry Murder went back to the other room. "The girl is elsewhere, but The Maitresse has what she needs."

Sentinel motioned the tall girl with a wave of the gun. "Go and sit on the bed, slutty girl. Next to your… man." She said the word 'man' as though she was describing a dog who had shit on the rug.

The Hands called to Mister Monoxide, "Your medicine, professor." Monoxide handed over his breathing mask to Zebra-Pants who, guided by The Hands, began inhaling. "That's it. Against your face. Breathe deeply." The boyfriend sucked poison and wilted. The tall girl started to shake at seeing him fade. She trembled, then began wailing as he softened under the effects of the gas.

"Be quiet, Girl." Mister Monoxide snapped. But beside her, Zebra-Pants suddenly convulsed and vomited into the mask.

The Hands let go of him with a retching sound of her own. "For Fuck's sake, I can taste it in my mouth."

The girl screamed, jumped to her feet and ran for the door. Mister Monoxide pushed her back but she grabbed at a table lamp and swung it hard, the heavy base smashing into his temple, his glasses flying from his face. He went down on one knee. Sentinel grabbed her hair as she swung the lamp a second time, crashing it onto Mister Monoxide as a brass hammer to the skull. She spun and swung the lamp at Sentinel, making her let go of her hair for a second. "Get her," Sentinel yelled. "Fucking get her." Sentinel grabbed for the girl again and gripped her collar, but the girl dipped lower whilst stepping one leg across the crouched Mister Monoxide. She slipped out of her T-shirt leaving Sentinel holding the empty garment. The girl burst out of the room and crashed against The Maitresse. Merry Murder jumped forward and got his arms around her waist, but she had the height advantage and pulled him with her to the kitchenette. She squirmed in his arms but he held fast. Then a toaster oven swung by him and grazed his ear. Then his hand started to hurt like fuck and he let go to see it bleeding. "What have you done?" He yelled.

The Maitresse yelled, "She's got a knife."

For a split-second the girl was in a powerful position. The Maitresse was backing against Nikki's room. Merry Murder was jumping back against the wall. Mister Monoxide was on his knees in the doorframe preventing those inside from giving immediate chase. The girl was tall and athletic. She wore only a pink thong but she wielded a six-inch kitchen knife and had blood across her breasts like war paint.

Pop-Pop

Two little holes opened over her breastbone. She stopped moving and glanced down, swaying a little. Smoke drifted from the barrel of Sentinel's pistol.

The girl fell. Her eyes rolled up to Merry Murder. Blood began streaming from her nose. "You fucking bitch." He kicked the knife away and hooked his arms under her shoulders, dragging her into Nikki's room as the blood from her nose began to pour like an open faucet. She was still moving when he closed the door but she wouldn't survive. "How is everything in there? Are you all okay?"

Mister Monoxide was crawling, sweeping his hand across the floor for his glasses. Sentinel found them. "I'm sorry, Professor. I had to shoot her. I didn't have a choice."

"There's no need to apologise. Maxine, are you alright?"

The Hands nodded to say she was fine, but her ashen skin said otherwise. "He vomited," she said thinly. "It broke my concentration and I could feel him dying. I felt the gas and the vomit all at once."

"Is he dead?"

The Hands checked Zebra-Pants. "Not yet."

"I'll finish him. The police will investigate, so let's not leave them a witness. Go outside and get some fresh air."

As The Hands shakily got to her feet she said, "You're bleeding, Professor. On your head."

Mister Monoxide wiped vomit from his mask with the corner of the bedspread. "I'll survive." Then to Zebra-Pants he whispered, "Unlike you." The boy's eyes were fluttering as the mask was pressed over his mouth. He breathed in and out in deep slow breaths for a minute, then the rising and falling of his chest became still.

By the time Zebra-Pants was dead the others,

except for Merry Murder, had left. The doctor had a tea towel wrapped around his hand. "Your head's bleeding."

Mister Monoxide gently felt his scalp. "I know. I'm going to have a bump. How about you, what happened to your hand?"

"The little bitch cut my fingers. Nothing major."

"Is she dead?"

Merry Murder opened the door to Nikki's room to check. "Sentinel hit her twice in the heart. It's a fucking mess. People will find this. We've got our DNA all over the place. You're bleeding, I'm bleeding. There's a shot girl and a gassed boyfriend." He made a sad little chuckle. "We're pretty lousy at this physical stuff."

"Thank the One True Lord that he sent us Sentinel."

The men descended the stairs to the ground floor. "Did you kill the kid in the kitchen?"

"No. He's just unconscious. I'll kill him. It'll only take a minute."

----- X -----

Luke Edwards was looking for a parking space when he caught sight of the old woman getting into the BMW by Nikki Bannister's house.

"No way. No fucking way you're here."

As the BMW departed, he swung around and took their parking spot. Had they seen him?

Further ahead he watched as the BMW turned the

148

corner into traffic.

They'd been here. They were obviously looking for Nikki, but why? His mind still fought to find a logical explanation. An explanation as to why Doctor Hill would lie to him. About how he said he was taking her to St. Ann's hospital and then had not taken her. About updating the records to discharge her. About the old woman saying 'We'll find the bitch' and being at her home; and most of all, about the black woman having, or possibly having a gun.

Was it all just paranoia? No. This wasn't paranoia, there were far too many red flags. But to cause an intrusion into business that wasn't his and challenge a senior doctor whilst still a junior was foolish. Evidence. Just observe and collect evidence.

Luke went to the home and rang the doorbells. "Come on, Nikki, answer the door." He called her again. It went to voicemail. "Nikki, this is Doctor Luke Edwards from the Complex Depression Unit. Please call me back as soon as you receive this, it's urgent."

What to do?

Where could she be?

What the hell could he do?

Then a thought. The cemetery. Yes, it was one of her favourite places. In fact her two suicide attempts were in the cemetery. She'd told him in the sessions how much she liked the place. She'd talked about how she liked to go there when she was upset or stressed.

Luke checked the map on his phone. The cemetery

was only a few hundred yards away.

----- X -----

The Maitresse was sitting in the front of the BMW as Sentinel drove. "She is this way. Somewhere over there," she pointed in the general direction. "And she's close."

"Can you sense anything else?"

"She's outdoors. There's a smell of foliage. Plants, trees and grass."

In the back seat The Hands was checking her mobile phone. "There's a park further to our right. Clissold Park. Take the next right."

Sentinel turned the car into the suburbs. "How far, Maxine?"

"Not far. Half a mile, maybe less."

The Maitresse nodded. "Yes. That could be it. It feels like she's in woodland."

----- X -----

Abney Park cemetery was populated by street drinkers. It was the sort of place where the unemployed could transition into being truly unemployable through alcohol. Everybody had a can of something. Some sat on benches, most sat on the ground. People were illuminated by their mobile phones.

It was dark, almost too dark to go into the cemetery proper. What the hell was he doing? Even if she was in there he'd never find her in the dark. Luke decided to walk the hundred yards or so to the chapel then call it a day. The cemetery had a romanticism to it, but he couldn't imagine Nikki wanting to be here when it was pitch black. If she wasn't amongst the drinkers by the entrance he would look no further.

----- X -----

"No. We're going the wrong way. She is behind us." The Maitresse was trying to twist in her seat.

Sentinel slowed the car. "Are you sure? The park is just here ahead of us."

"It feels like she is in a park, but I'm almost certain she's in that direction." The Maitresse pointed back between the seats. "The little bitch has us running around in circles."

The Hands worked her mobile phone. "There's a cemetery behind us. That's the only other place with trees and foliage like you're describing."

"Then I want to try there."

Sentinel turned the car. "Okay, let's go back."

As the car aligned, The Maitresse called out, "Yes. I have her. She's ahead of us." She pointed through the window. "She's not moving. There's real anguish to this girl."

"Ha," Sentinel coughed a short laugh. "I'll give her some fucking anguish."

----- X -----

The cemetery chapel looked like a small medieval castle with an unusually large spire. There were more street drinkers congregating around the building. "Jesus," Luke mumbled to himself. "This place is a magnet to alcoholics." He looked over the little groups, hearing a multitude of languages from East European to what he assumed was Turkish and finally poverty-class English, but Nikki wasn't here. Or if she was, he wasn't going to find her in the dark.

He'd tried.

As he headed back along the main route to the entrance, he saw them. The old woman was leading the way. There were overhead lights at the entrance and Luke was in darkness, so he knew they hadn't seen him. He backtracked to the chapel and retreated into the shadows, crouching low to conceal himself.

The old woman led the way. The younger woman switched on her mobile phone light to shine ahead. The black woman did likewise.

"This way," he heard the old woman say.

Luke whispered to himself, "What the hell are you people doing?" He followed, sheepishly at first, until he thought he lost sight of them. There were twists and turns to the pathways and the whole place was overgrown and reclaimed by nature. Luke tried to cut between headstones but the climbing ivy was wrapped around the masonry and tangled underfoot like he was walking through fishing nets.

The deeper they went into the cemetery the darker it became until the path had almost vanished from view and all that could be seen were the occasional flickers of their phones used to light the way.

Then Luke heard the old woman say, "There she is." His heart pounded. They stopped moving. What was he supposed to do now? Go out and confront them? He moved closer as silently as possible, then froze when he heard the voice of Doctor Hill whispering something.

"Hello, Nikki." Doctor Hill's voice was bizarrely seductive and it seemed to vibrate through his bones. "You ran away from me, but it's time to come back. Come to me. Come to your doctor."

Luke felt the warmth in the voice, the sensuousness.

Then a tiny voice said, "You injected me. You did something to me and tried to drown me." It was Nikki. He couldn't see her, but she was crazy close. Literally within a few feet of him. Her words were spoken like a child.

"That was in the past, Nikki. I wouldn't want to hurt you. I think something happened. Something with the medication that has left you confused and unhappy. Are you unhappy, Nikki?"

There was the sound of soft crying. "Yes."

"Then come to me, Nikki. Come to me and I will take all the sadness away."

Luke held his breath. He wanted to hear everything

but his heart was pounding so strongly it was thumping in his eardrums.

"I'm frightened," Nikki whispered.

"I know you're frightened. I think the medication gave you terrible visions. They gave you dreams and nightmares. I think you've had a terrible time and I want to help you get better. There's no need to be frightened now, Nikki. Come to me. Come to me, now."

Then with a fright at how close she was, Nikki Bannister climbed off a tomb about four feet high and capped with an angel holding a sword. She was barely ten feet away with Doctor Hill and his group on the far side.

As she reached them she yelped in pain like a dog with a stepped-on tail.

"Be careful." It was Doctor Hill, now speaking in his normal voice. "The dumb cow slashed her own wrist. Don't let the handcuffs tear open the wound. Not yet."

Luke's legs turned to jelly. He heard that. He heard it plain as day. He pulled tighter into his crouch, clinging to the edge of the stonework and hiding behind the gravestone as Doctor Hill and his friends led Nikki Bannister away in handcuffs. He gave them a head start then broke out onto a pathway to follow under cover of darkness. They still used their phones as torches but even in the dark he could see Nikki's hands were behind her back and the young woman was gripping her cuffed wrist.

"Jesus, this is wrong," Luke whispered. "This is fucked up."

They moved quickly past the street drinkers and along the avenue of graves towards the entrance arch. Luke worked his mobile phone. Nine, nine, nine. "Emergency. Which service, please?"

"I need the police."

Nikki was marched to the entrance and Luke had to run to catch up. He ran fast, trying to hold his phone to his ear. He burst out through the arch onto Stoke Newington High Street and saw Nikki stepping into the back of a white van. Her hands were visibly cuffed; he was seeing it with his own eyes. This was a kidnapping and he had to act.

----- X -----

"Hey! Hey, stop!" Luke screamed as loud as he could and sprinted towards Nikki and her abductors. "Let her go." Mister Monoxide glared at him.

Merry Murder called his name, "Luke?"

"I said let her go. Nikki. Nikki, are you okay?"

Luke dropped his phone into his pocket, still connecting to the police. He would shout and hopefully be heard.

The Hands stepped into his path. Luke tried to brush her aside but she got her palm to his throat and he stopped in his tracks. "Is this the boy from your hospital?"

"Yes, it is. What the fuck are you doing here, Luke?"

He gasped for breath. He was unable to get the words out. It was like the woman holding his throat had hold of his entire nervous system. He was frozen in place and barely able to breathe. He wanted to shout. He wanted to push her away, but he just couldn't move.

"I said, what are you doing here?" Merry Murder asked again.

Luke felt a pain squeezing in his stomach and his larynx open up as though he was being forced to expel air. "I'm trying to save Nikki."

"To save her?" The Hands quizzed.

"We can't do this here, people are watching." Mister Monoxide waved them towards the van. "Put him in the vehicle. We'll kill him elsewhere."

The Hands whispered, "Get in, you little prick." Luke complied unsure how or why. His body was doing whatever she commanded whilst his brain was trying to make it stop. He climbed into the van and sat against the wall beside Nikki.

The Maitresse was in there too, holding on to Nikki by the elbow. "Who is he?" she asked.

"It's Peter's workmate. Says he came to rescue the girl."

The Maitresse bit her teeth together, a flash of rage showing. "Oh, you fucking imbecile. I don't know what you think you're doing, but I promise, once I've dealt with this little bitch I'm going to nail your balls to the floor. You stupid, stupid, fucking little shit."

Sentinel appeared at the door. "What's

happening?"

"We've got ourselves a white knight. Some little faggot just tried to rescue the girl."

"Have you got him? Shall I kill him now?"

Mister Monoxide took a breath from his mask, "Let's get out of here first. We'll dispose of him later."

Nikki suddenly snapped out of her hypnosis. "What's happening?"

Merry Murder leaned in through the door with a smile and whispered with his golden tones. "It's all right, Nikki. Everything is fine."

Sentinel said, "If you take the van to Almassy I'll follow you." She pointed at Luke and said, "But if that little shit causes trouble just let him escape and I'll cut him down wherever we are." Sentinel slammed the loading door closed.

Mister Monoxide and Merry Murder got into the front seats. "Just sit there nice and quietly, Nikki," the doctor called out with his special voice, "this will all be over soon." Without his special voice he said to Luke, "You fucked. Do you know that? You really fucked up."

"What's…" Luke's vocal chords tightened and his breathing froze.

The Hands pulled closer to him and whispered, "Don't say a word."

Merry Murder stared into Luke's eyes. "You shouldn't have done this, Luke. You're going to fucking die for it.

CHAPTER NINE

The Hands kept firm hold of Luke as he was marched through the lobby of Almassy House. In the office, Luke glanced at his surroundings. The mahogany desks, the bookcases of law texts. There was only one exit and he prepared himself to try for it given half a chance.

Nikki had her hands cuffed behind her back and made no sign of distress. Although she looked miserable and lost, she didn't manifest the horror of someone being taken against their will.

"I'll put the cuffs on this intrusive cunt. He seems more trouble than the sow." The Maitresse moved behind Nikki and used a small key to unfasten the cuffs. They looked old, like those carried by Victorian policemen. She prodded at Nikki's stitches. "My goodness. How did you end up like this?"

Nikki didn't seem to register the question.

"She cut herself," Merry Murder said. "She tried to kill herself and failed."

"Never mind, Dear. We will succeed where you didn't. We're very good at it. We're experts."

The Hands physically controlled Luke to turn him into a statue. He could feel beads of sweat forming on his brow and his lip trembled as he tried to break the bond.

He mustered all his willpower and concentrated on wiggling his fingertips but the moment he thought he could he inexplicably lost all sensation in his arms.

The Maitresse cuffed Luke's hands behind his back, the locking bar clicking over the ratchet until painfully tight and cutting off the circulation. Doctor Hill lifted Nikki's chin and stood close enough to kiss her. "We're going to ask you some questions, Nikki; and you're going to talk to us." His words were anaesthetising, each sentence hissing like a snake that hypnotized the listener. "You will enjoy answering our questions."

Behind them Merry Murder opened the bookcase door to the staircase and as The Hands turned her head to look, she momentarily let her touch fall away from Luke's wrist.

It was all the break he needed.

"You people are fucking crazy." Luke ran towards the exit with his wrists cuffed behind his back. Mister Monoxide tried to block him. "Get out of my fucking way!" He charged at the old man but Sentinel was out of the chair in a flash and chopped him in the throat with the edge of her hand, the blow smashing his larynx. Her jacket flashed aside and the gun came out. She pushed him to his knees with the fluid moves of a martial artist. She stood over him, gripping his hair and pressing the muzzle to his neck.

"The only reason I haven't shot you," she said, "is because I don't want to get blood on the carpet."

"Perhaps he needs a little medicine," Mister Monoxide said. "Just a taste." From his coat he brought the breathing mask. "Do you see what I'm holding? This is carbon monoxide, my friend. A few breaths of this can cause irreparable brain damage." He held the mask close to Luke's face. "I think a little taste will make you far less excitable."

"Okay, I'm sorry." Luke pushed away from the mask as it was pressed to his face. "No!" Luke yelled and twisted his head. He tried to stand but Sentinel held him firm and Monoxide pressed the mask over his mouth and nose. He held his breath, squeezing his eyes closed.

"Is he holding his breath?"

"He is trying."

Luke felt Sentinel grip his hair tighter. She pulled his head straight and pressed the gun painfully into a pressure point by his collar bone. "Stop resisting," Monoxide said. "You'll be surprised how sweet the sensation is." Luke's lungs burned. He fought to hold off but his body tried to squeeze in some air through the corner of his lips, sipping in gently, as though breathing through pursed lips would somehow purify what he was getting. He coughed out and took a partial breath. It didn't hurt. He didn't taste or smell anything. Maybe it was a joke. A ruse or a trick to panic him. A flash thought went through his head of something he knew of psychological trickery. Islamist prisoners at Guantanamo Bay were awoken by faceless guards in riot gear who pinned them down whilst a nurse injected them from a mysterious hypodermic. The syringe contained harmless saline, but the psychological impact of being injected against your will was what he was facing now. Was it real?

The old man spoke his words slowly. "Breathe it, you fucker." Luke couldn't hold out any longer and took a breath. He had to pray it was the Guantanamo ruse. He purged and took a deeper breath much to the old man's delight. "That's right, you bastard, take your medicine."

Luke made two deep breaths before the mask was taken away. He immediately felt light headed. His heart pounded in his ears and the centre of gravity shifted making him feel like he was falling towards the corner of the room. He hadn't tasted or smelled anything in the gas but it was potent. Something in it pulled him towards docility. He felt himself being lifted and struggled to put his feet under him. He saw a bookcase melt away to a stone staircase. He stumbled and tripped on the stairs, falling hard against his face. His brow hit the ground hard. Then he was back to his feet, or his knees. He could feel a strange sensation of pins and needles in his fingertips. Then it was dark and he was in a tight cavernous tunnel. It was steep. Leading down into darkness with a string of bulbs overhead. He steadied himself against the wall and gasped for breath. His head throbbed from the fall. He was sweating profusely and felt an overwhelming desire to lay down and sleep. The descent took forever. At the bottom, Luke dropped to his knees and fell forward. His collar was grabbed to pull him back to his knees. The world was spinning like he was so drunk he would pass out. He saw himself pushed towards the open door of a vestibule of bare rock. The door closed behind him and he dropped to his knees. It was dark except for the line of light spilling below the door. Now he fell forward and rolled onto his side. His hands in the cuffs felt completely numb. His head hung awkwardly onto the stone floor, but it was peaceful enough to rest. To sleep.

----- X -----

"Tell this lady about the man you were with last night." Mister Monoxide was motioning to The Maitresse Bathory. Nikki was sitting on the floor as her interrogators stood in a circle around her, all except for The Maitresse Bathory who sat demurely in a chair, her persona returned to village parishioner.

"I don't know what to say about him. I don't know him."

Merry Murder crouched beside Nikki. "Listen to my voice," he spoke with the hypnotic tones again. "I want you to be happy and the best way to be happy is to tell us about the man who took you from my house."

Her head rocked from side to side. "I don't know him."

"Do you know his name?"

She paused for a moment. "Yes. He said he called himself Mister Deathmask."

Merry Murder looked to The Maitresse.

"Anything?"

"No. I need more."

Merry Murder whispered his velvet tones some more. "Where did you go, Nikki? When you left my home, where did you go."

"To his house."

"Where?"

"Finchley. I don't know exactly. But when I left, I found the Underground station at Finchley."

"Describe what happened," The Maitresse said. "Tell me everything."

Nikki did. She felt in a dream world. She felt without control, being carried towards whatever destination these people had in store for her… except, there was something else… there was a sensation that she wasn't alone. "He took me in a car," she was saying, "He had a garage for the car, away from the house. We had to walk. He give me his shoes. He made me wear them so I wouldn't hurt my feet."

"You wore his shoes?" The Maitresse asked. "Was this last night?"

Nikki shrugged. "Last night. I wore his shoes."

The Maitresse got out of her chair. "Show me her feet. Show me the soles of her feet." Merry Murder and Sentinel grabbed Nikki's ankles and lifted her, rolling the girl onto her back as they pulled off her shoes. She was wearing the dress that Mister Deathmask had brought her, but she wasn't wearing underwear and her hands instinctively grabbed the fabric to cover her crotch, but with her ankles held in the air she was exposed and squirming. "Hold her," The Maitresse commanded. She pressed the tip of her nose to the soles of Nikki's feet. "Yes... Yes... I can smell him." The Maitresse stepped away and paced the cavern for a few moments. "Perhaps I can find him. If he is in Finchley. If I get close to him, I will find him."

"Finchley is a big place," Mister Monoxide added. He addressed Nikki directly, "Tell me, Girl. Describe the area of the house you were at."

Nikki was still on her back with her feet held in the air. "It's a broken house. The windows are broken. The garden is overgrown. It's a mess."

"Is it a terraced house? A suburb? Is it a busy area or a quiet location?"

"Quiet, I guess. It was dark. I didn't see. It had a front and back garden and I think it was detached. Or maybe semi-detached... I don't know. It was dark when he took me."

Nikki felt calm. She felt really calm.

Magdalena was here.

She wasn't visible, but she was here and watching. She was right here and Nikki felt the ghostly girl was in some way controlling or manipulating the proceedings. Magdalena was working through her. She was inside her mind, she was putting the words into her mouth and she had these people exactly where she wanted them.

----- X -----

"Don't forget what I said about your guns." Sentinel was giving them a new round of instruction. "Only shoot if your life is directly threatened. Remember, we must deliver him alive. He's worthless if he dies."

"We are at your command," Mister Monoxide said. "Lead us as you see fit."

Sentinel, The Maitresse and The Hands took the BMW, whilst Mister Monoxide and Merry Murder took the van. Merry Murder would drive.

Mister Monoxide took a long inhalation from his mask. "I feel exhilarated. Our mission is almost complete. We have our quarry and our warrior princess to capture him. I never imagined a moment like this. I never imagined a moment where the goal was in sight."

Merry Murder hummed an acknowledgement. "Are you scared of what comes next? Are you scared of how we will be judged?"

Mister Monoxide shook his head vigorously and took an added inhalation from his mask. "Not at all." He leaned across and gave Merry Murder a firm pat on the arm. "We have done well, my friend. All of Hell will hold us in esteem."

----- X -----

"Doctor Edwards? Doctor Edwards, wake up." She was in some kind of vestibule, locked in with the doctor.

It was now that the fear was hitting her. She'd watched everything happen as though it was a peaceful dream. She was in Abney park cemetery when Doctor Hill came and spoke to her. She knew he'd tried to drown her, yet for some reason she couldn't comprehend, she'd gone back to him. Trusted him. How the hell could she trust him? He tried to drown her. Fucking drown her? Jesus, fucking Christ, why on Earth would she go to him after that? Why allow the old woman to put handcuffs on her? Why had she done that?

In complete darkness, she heard the doctor groan. "Who is it?" he slurred.

"Doctor Edwards? It's Nikki. Nikki Bannister, do you remember?" Her mouth felt dry and her words came out too fast. Why was he here? She remembered seeing Doctor Hill angry at him. She had sat with him in the van. What the hell? The whole thing was flooding back as a sequence of events she recalled with absolute clarity, yet she couldn't understand why she'd gone along with these people. "Doctor Edwards? Doctor Edwards, can you hear me?" As she said it her voice trailed into the high notes.

"Phoooo in pork it."

"What?"

"Phooone. Phooone"

"A phone? Telephone. Do you have a phone?" Nikki's hands reached to the doctor in darkness. She felt his hair, she felt the plastic arm of his glasses behind his ear, the spectacles still on his face. She ran her hands over his shoulder and down to his cuffed hands. "Where is it?" Then almost shouting. "Where is it? Where is the phone?"

"Pork it."

"Pork… pocket? POCKET!" Her hands rushed around his suit to the outside pockets. "I FOUND IT!" she yelled. "You need to roll over, you're lying on it." The doctor seemed to be mustering some strength and clarity of mind. He was behaving like a drunk who had just woken but was on the verge of passing out again. Nikki put both hands on his chest and pressed with all her weight to roll him. The strain pulled at the stitches in her wrist. She got her hand under him and yanked at his jacket. "I've got it. I've got it!"

The doctor slurred his response. "Call pleeee."

Nikki found the power button in the dark and the screen came to life. The screen had cracked but the phone was alive and the light was her candle. The phone was on a lock-screen but it could make emergency calls. Then her heart sank. They were underground. "There's no signal," she whispered to the doctor. "We can't call for help, they brought us into an underground cave."

Beside her the doctor opened his eyes a little wider and slurred the words, "Help me sssit uuup."

----- X -----

Mister Deathmask was awakened by a dream of Magdalena. He was watching her dance through an English garden of green lawns and flowers. She was in sunshine, her white dress flowing behind her. In his dream she still had no eyes but his subconscious mind edited the imagination so skilfully that he never had to look at her disfigurement. Her hair would be blowing across her face, or her back was turned to him.

In the dream, Magdalena rushed towards him until her eyeless face was barely inches from his. "They're coming for you. Be ready. I cannot help you now, I must hold my strength. They will try and take you. They're going to try and deliver you to Leonora. This is our chance, my love. This is our chance."

Deathmask sprung from the mattress. Plaster cast faces hung from the walls. A single candle burning to light the room. He was dressed in his sweat worn slacks and a cream coloured shirt with a filthy collar. He grabbed his nearby fuel can and felt the weight. Ready. The brass garden spray was full of petrol. He pumped it quickly, building the pressure then slung it across his shoulders. He grabbed his coat and threaded the spray nozzle through the sleeve as he put it on. He grabbed his mask and hat. He put on his gloves and brass knuckles. It was fast. He was fast. Ready and prepared from sleeping to a fighting stance in thirty seconds.

On the dresser was the knife, the Eye of Magdalena, he held it for a moment then left it in place. Hopefully, he would get to exact Magdalena's revenge in similar fashion. Hopefully, he could blind one or two of them, gouge out their eyes before casting their faces as a treat for her.

He moved from the bedroom to the bottom of the

stairs. The front door was barricaded, the back door was unlocked. He thought about it for a moment, then went through the kitchen to open the door wide as an invitation.

He returned to the foot of the stairs.

Mister Deathmask waited in the dark, wearing his devil mask and bowler hat.

The people coming had one access point. When they came they could fight with him; they might win, they might kill him, but he was ready for the fight.

----- X -----

They drove through Finchley from one end to the other. The Maitresse sat up front beside Sentinel, breathing slowly with her eyes closed, concentrating. "I can sense him, but there's too much noise," she said. "It's like trying to concentrate in a discotheque when what I need is a library."

"Is there anything we can do to help?"

"I need somewhere quiet. Away from people. Maybe a rooftop if it's high enough."

In the back seat, The Hands was scouring the map on her mobile phone. "There's an open space on East End Road. I think it's a cricket club." Sentinel glanced at The Maitresse who made a sharp nod. "Keep going straight. You need to turn right before East Finchley station." Sentinel kept the BMW on course. They found East End Road. "It's coming up on the right." There was a cricket training centre and a wide-open cricket pitch.

"Leave me to do this alone," The Maitresse said. She got out of the car and walked onto the deserted field. Behind them the van carrying Merry Murder and Mister Monoxide approached.

The Hands got out of the car to talk with them. "She wants to be alone."

"How's it going? Can she find him?"

"I don't know. She just wanted some space. She said there was too much noise."

Far out on the field, The Maitresse stopped walking and became a statue.

Then somebody else was walking to her, a man holding a glass of beer. The Hands ran out towards the drinking man. As she covered the ground, she saw a small bar to the side of the club with a patio overlooking the field. The drinker had been here, he'd seen The Maitresse walking onto the crease in darkness. "Are you okay, Love?" the man called. He had silver hair and a bulbous nose.

"Get away from her," The Hands called.

"Oh, 'ello, what's all these women doing on the field at night?" The man sounded jolly and friendly.

The Hands grabbed his wrist. "Turn around and walk back to the bar, Grandad."

"Aye, alright," the man turned on a sixpence and went straight back in whilst The Hands kept hold of him. "And what's your name?" he asked. The Hands didn't answer. She walked him briskly to the patio then took control of his bladder until he was bursting, crossing his legs and starting to double over. "Arhh, I think I need to go to the toilet, Love."

"Go on then."

The man ran, or rather skipped with his knees locked together as fast as he could. She turned back to watch The Maitresse, still standing at the crease in the middle of an empty field. She remained there for at least a minute then headed back. The Hands walked out to meet her. "Can you sense him?"

"Faintly. I know the direction. It's hard to follow, but I think I've got him."

----- X -----

In the caverns, Luke was groggy with the worst hangover he'd ever felt. His head pounded and he felt super dehydrated, his lungs felt inefficient and couldn't suck up enough air, but his strength was coming back as his bone marrow worked overtime to produce new red blood cells.

"Doctor Edwards, we're trapped in here. We're locked in."

He'd managed to get almost seated against the wall but he was still slouched at an awkward angle. Drowsily and feeling like he would vomit, he said, "Shine the light."

Nikki used the phone screen to try and illuminate the cell but it went off every few seconds.

"Password," he slurred. "One, one, two, two."

Nikki hit the broken screen with the entry code and the phone functions appeared. She knew how it worked, quickly finding the flashlight app. "They brought us underground. I think they've gone. They're looking for the man who rescued me last night."

"The door?" His head drooped to the side as he said it.

"It's like iron, it doesn't move at all."

"Are there hinges? Any joins?" His voice slurred badly.

Nikki shone the light around the doorframe. "No, look, there's nothing." She shone the light around the vestibule. It was a prison cell cut into the bedrock, six feet high and five feet deep. Nikki knelt in front of him. "We can't get out."

----- X -----

"This is the way, I can feel him ahead of us, but drive slowly. I don't want to go around in circles." Sentinel had the car at a crawl, barely making five miles an hour. They were in leafy suburbs with cars parked along both sides. "Slow… go slower."

Sentinel brought the car to an almost halt. "Maybe you should walk? So that you're free of distractions."

"Yes. Stop the car. He's close. Very close." Sentinel waited for The Maitresse to get out. "Don't lag too far. I have a feeling he's prepared for us. I can sense he is like a coiled snake. This man is unusual and I won't be able to defend myself as well as you."

Sentinel looked to The Hands in the back seat. "Maxine, you drive. I want to be on the street behind Marigold. Stay back about thirty feet."

They switched places.

Standing outside, Sentinel made eye-contact with Mister Monoxide in the van as it pulled up behind. She touched her thumb and finger together to signify things were okay. "How far away do you think he is? Can you estimate?"

The Maitresse breathed deeply as though scenting the air. "He's not far. We're within a few hundred yards of him. She began walking forward. "I do appreciate you coming with me. I'm afraid of this man."

"I'm not going to let him hurt you, Marigold. If you see him, run behind me. I'll do the rest."

They continued on a road darkened by overhanging trees that blocked the street lights. It was preternaturally quiet. No car engines. No TV noise from the houses or children playing. No wildlife. Sentinel held her breath for a moment so as not to miss the sound of something, or some clue to movement; but the only sound that came was when Maxine started the engine to continue forward.

They walked a few minutes more when The Maitresse suddenly stopped, her feet stomping slightly with the action. "He's ahead of us. He's waiting but he's bored. I think he's been waiting a long time and has gotten complacent."

"How far away is he?"

The Maitresse pointed to a house hidden behind an overgrown privet hedgerow. "He's in there."

----- X -----

Luke was on his knees with a shoulder against the door. The door was as unmoving as Nikki had said but he had to try and force it. In his weakened state the best he could do was lay on his back and kick at it with both feet at once. Although it was made of wood, it hurt his feet as though he'd kicked a rock at full force.

"What happened to you?" he asked weakly. "Doctor Hill was supposed to take you to the hospital. I called, but they said you weren't there."

"He injected me in the car. He injected me with something that made me tired and forgetful. When I woke up I was in a water tank in his house."

"A water tank?"

Nikki was sat against the wall. She pulled her knees against her chest and wrapped her arms around them. "I was naked in this tank and it started filling with water. I could see him on the other side of the glass. He was drinking wine. I think he wanted to watch me drown."

Luke sat straighter, the confession somehow shocking some life into him. "Jesus Christ. Doctor Hill?"

"I would have drowned, but this man came and rescued me. He fought with the doctor and set the house on fire. I nearly drowned but he…" Nikki's eyes pulled back as though she was fixated on a vision in her own mind.

"What is it?"

Nikki's eyes glassed over as though she was about to cry. "Did I die?"

"What?"

She squeezed her eyes closed. "I was drowning, then a man rescued me. There were flames everywhere. The man took me to a house where a little girl came to me. A ghost girl without eyes." Her voice went high as emotion flooded her speech. "She told me to kill myself… Am I dead? Did I drown? Am I in hell, now? I'm surrounded by monstrous people and ghostly girls and… and…" Tears flooded now. "I'm locked up. I'm locked in a fucking cave by the same doctor who tried to drown me." The tears came out with wails of anguish. She stood and slammed herself at the door. "Let me out. Let me out. Please. Please. I can't do this anymore. Let me out!"

----- X -----

Sentinel organised them. "Maitresse, Professor, I want you to stay in the garden. Have your weapons to hand but keep them hidden. We don't want anybody to come past and see you." Mister Monoxide tipped his head to acknowledge. "Maxine, I want you to go first so you can lay your hands on him. I'll be behind you." She handed one of the tasers to her. "This is just a precaution. You only get one shot so be careful. I'm going to be beside you."

The Hands was looking between Sentinel and Mister Monoxide, her brow was furrowed and her usual swagger had deserted her. "Okay. Okay, I'll do it."

Sentinel held her own taser and the target pistol. "I'll be right behind you. If you feel me pressing your shoulder down, drop to one knee and I'll shoot across you. Just get your hands on him."

Sentinel led the way. The front was shrouded in overgrown hedgerow that concealed most of the house. The front door was blocked with boxes and refuse and the junk was spilling out into the garden. She looked back to Mister Monoxide and The Maitresse and pointed to the front lawn. They took their places.

The Maitresse whispered, "He's in there."

Sentinel continued toward the rear. The back door was open. She stepped in silently and looked across the kitchen. It was dark. No lights on in the house. There was a table and two chairs but little else. "Maxine," she whispered. "Come in. You go first." The Hands stepped forward. "I'll protect you," she whispered again. "You just grab the fucker."

They went into a darkened hallway with a staircase. Sentinel looked to the top of the stairs through the bannister railings. Nothing. She edged The Hands forward towards a door on the left. The room was empty. There were French doors looking out into the back garden but no furniture or carpet.

Sentinel backed them out and looked across her shoulder to Merry Murder who was leaning against the wall with his arms tight to his chest and the little silver revolver pointed to the ceiling. He was sweating, his breathing rapid. "Stay cool," she whispered.

They crept towards the front room, the door still closed. She could feel Maxine trembling. "I won't let anything happen to you," she whispered. "Open the door and push it all the way. I'm right behind you."

The Hands turned the doorknob and pushed. There was no rush of action, no sudden onslaught. The room had just enough moonlight spilling in to show it was as barren as the last. No furniture, no carpet and no Son of Light.

"Upstairs." Sentinel whispered. "We need to check upstairs." She turned The Hands and pointed her at the staircase.

The floorboards creaked with each step. "Oh, shit."

Sentinel leaned close. "Keep moving."

It was tight on the staircase.

The top of the stairs had a blind corner.

Then something spooked The Hands. Sentinel felt her freeze up. She even held her breath, perhaps to listen more intently. Perhaps it was the Son of Light or perhaps it was the sound of the floorboards, but something made her lock up. Sentinel pointed the pistol past her to cover the way, demonstrating by action that she would protect. Nerves. It was only nerves. The Hands was frightened and had stopped to calm herself. Sentinel tapped her arm to usher her forward but she didn't move. Something really had spooked her. In her quietest voice she whispered, "Maxine, move forward," but she didn't. Their position was tactically dangerous. Bunched together on a staircase. They had the advantage and were five against one, but on a staircase and facing a blind corner was the worst place to freeze up. "Maxine you need to…"

…Something came around the corner. Something high up that caught a sparkle of moonlight. It was a human hand and for a split second Sentinel imagined it was a grenade coming her way. The worst possible thing in their location. Her gift of deadshot kicked in and the world dropped into slow motion. She saw with a sudden clarity and sense of purpose. The muscles of her legs were already throwing her aside to get a clean shot. She could see the hand pointing from around the corner. Something came from it, not a grenade but liquid. It squirted hard, under pressure. In the same slow motion she saw Maxine raising the taser, the red dot of the built-in laser rushing up each step as her arms arced upward. She started pushing The Hands aside as the liquid sprayed across her. She lined up the target pistol unsure what she was aiming at. Was it a snake? Something was spitting around the corner. Liquid. The red dot of Maxine's laser sight was moving to the corner but there was no target in view. It was just a hand spraying something on her. Something that smelled… petrol… it wasn't a grenade it was petrol and it was splashing off Maxine's face and chest, blowing into her eyes. The red beam of the laser moved close but there was no target in sight.

"MAXINE!"

Petrol.

The taser.

"DON'T…"

In the same slow-motion she saw the taser front burst with glittering confetti as the two electrified probes shot out. She had a moment to see electricity arc. The taser would miss. The Son of Light was hidden behind a wall. But it didn't matter. There was petrol in the air. An aerosolized spray of high octane fuel about to be ignited by the electrodes.

There was a moment where time slowed enough she could see the fireball beginning. She managed a single shot from the target pistol that ricocheted off what looked like a brass glove. She'd hit the retreating hand right as the fireball was about to burst. To Sentinel's mind it seemed there was a second to appreciate the horror, but when it came it snapped her perception of time back to normal with an almighty fucking bang.

The aerosolised fuel exploded in a ball of yellow and orange flame that rushed towards them then exploded again as The Hands, covered in liquid fuel, burst into flames with a glass shattering scream. Sentinel pulled her back but she was already throwing herself away, the flames from her clothing licking up the walls and spreading across the ceiling.

Then the Son of Light rounded the corner and jumped forward with both feet aimed at The Hands' flaming chest. Sentinel swung the pistol, trying to pick out a weak spot but it was too fast. The Son of Light's boots connected with The Hands to kick both her and Sentinel backwards down the stairs. Sentinel felt herself weightless for a second before hitting the floor and dropping her weapons. The screaming and flaming Hands was on top of her. The fire from her hair and clothing so powerful she became a black silhouette inside the fireball, scrambling and clawing at herself as she screamed. Sentinel tried to push her off, but The Hands was panicking, flailing her arms. The Son of Light careened through the air, leaping from the top of the stairs to smash his boots into her face.

He was like a gargoyle. A red grinning face. A bowler hat and a black coat that trailed behind him like a cape as he leapt through the flames.

She glanced aside and saw Merry Murder aim his pistol at the Son of Light. Despite the confusion he remembered to aim low, but the Son of Light was just too quick and grabbed his wrist. The gun fired and the bullet hit the floor, the shock wave hitting Sentinel as much as the kick down the stairs.

"MAXINE, GET OFF!"

Flames were spreading up the stairs.

She pushed The Hands aside, who by now had most of her clothes burned off. She was still on fire.

Sentinel looked for her guns. The Son of Light swung a punch into Merry Murder and caught him square on the jaw with brass knuckles. The doctor was going to get the shit kicked out of him for a second time. She saw the target pistol and dove for the weapon, already seeing the chain of actions on how she would grab it and turn. From the corner of her eye she picked out the side of the Son of Light's right knee as her target, but seemingly to counteract her move, he began turning away. Get the gun. Do whatever it takes. Her fingers wrapped around the pistol and her body turned as she saw the Son of Light point the snake at her. He was going to spray again. With only a split second to decide she pushed backwards as the fuel sprayed.

It hit Maxine again. Another dose of flaming petrol hit her in the face and engulfed her in a scorching fireball. The burning woman let out another agonising scream, jumped to her feet and began a flaming dance, swinging her arms and kicking her legs as her limbs dragged trails of fire.

Then she saw Mister Monoxide rush in behind the Son of Light. He wrapped his whole arm around their target's neck and pulled off his red face. Merry Murder was on his knees but used his strength to grab the Son of Light's legs as Monoxide pressed his own poison mask against Mister Deathmask's face.

The Son of Light slowed.

Merry Murder pulled his arms tight around Deathmask's legs. The Hands collapsed by the foot of the stairs with her blackened arms slowly clawing through the fire that surrounded them. Sentinel had her gun aimed, ready to shoot, but the professor had done it. The Son of Light was fading. He dropped to his knees, the poison was working.

Mister Monoxide yelled, "Maitresse. We need your restraints."

Merry Murder climbed from beneath Deathmask and knelt across his back as the Maitresse brought her manacles.

As the handcuffs clicked into place, Mister Monoxide ran to The Hands and used his overcoat to beat the flames, then covered her entirely to smother the fire. When he took the fabric away her wide-open eyes stared through a charred face. "Don't let me die," she rasped. "Don't let me die before he is delivered."

"Where is the bathroom?" the Professor asked. "Sentinel? The bathroom."

"I don't know. It must be upstairs."

Mister Monoxide pressed his arms under The Hands and lifted her charred body. Her clothes were almost entirely burned away and he saw the mark of the One True Lord on her breast, an angry red pentagram within the circle. It seemed to glow around the blackened and puffed skin. "Stay strong, Child. I think the One True Lord is with you."

"I can feel him." The skin of her face was mostly black with angry red cracks where the fat under the skin had bubbled. Her eyes had gone milky, with the iris bleached white and the pupil whitened to a cataract. "I can feel him with me."

Mister Monoxide kicked open a door. A room filled with faces and a single candle. He kicked open another door and discovered the bathroom. He dumped The Hands into the tub, practically dropping her. He turned on the light by a pull cord then turned on the shower from the cold water tap. Water sprayed onto the charred woman making her shriek and arch her back. He turned the water higher to full power. The running cold water would take some of the heat out of the burn, but this was a mortal wound. No ordinary human could survive this, but again he saw the pentagram on her breast appear to glow an angry red and he felt the One True Lord looking over them.

"Get him to The Secretary," The Hands rasped. The shower water was splashing off her face. She grabbed the hand of Mister Monoxide to pull him closer. "Get that fucker to The Secretary before I die."

Mister Monoxide held on to her hand. "You need a hospital."

"No. The One True Lord is with me. He protects me, but you must be fast. Get that mother fucker to The Secretary now."

----- X -----

In the hallway, Sentinel was straddled across Mister Deathmask's back and had his cuffed hands twisted upwards in a stress position, wrenching his shoulders ninety degrees backwards. The guy stunk of stale sweat and made grunting snores in his semi-conscious state.

Merry Murder was struggling to assemble the bondage pole. The Maitresse Bathory was standing over them with a roll of duct tape. "Put the poll under the cuffs," The Maitresse said. "Then tape him to it. Tape it around his neck, his waist and his ankles."

Merry Murder threaded the pole through his cuffed arms. He got to work wrapping the Son of Light's ankles to the pipework then did likewise on his knees and passed the roll of tape to Sentinel who did the same to his neck, stringing him up like a lynching. Within minutes he was handcuffed and wrapped to the pole like he was on a roasting spit. "Where is Maxine?"

Sentinel grimaced and shook her head. The Maitresse gestured upstairs. "The professor took her upstairs."

Merry Murder said, "We're going to need everybody to carry this bastard to the van. Can you see if they're ready to come?"

The Maitresse made her way upstairs and saw Mister Monoxide standing in the doorway to the front bedroom. "Professor?"

He took a long and deep draw from his poison mask. "Look at this." She joined him in the front bedroom as he pointed to one of the plaster casts on the wall. The face was bloated with morbid obesity.

"Is that Charles?"

"It is The Pain. Wounded. Screaming."

"So, the Son of Light is a sculptor. I will break his hands for what he has done, I will cut off his fingers and thumbs."

"They're not sculptures, they're casts. They're death masks."

The Maitresse visibly shuddered. "I dread to think that he had this planned for you and I." Mister Monoxide pointed to the ornate blade on the dresser. "Oh, my… is that what I think it is?"

"It is."

The Maitresse picked it up, treating the object with absolute respect and began reading the inscriptions carved into the handle. "Does it say which of the twelve?"

"Magdalena."

The Maitresse repeated the name in a whisper. "Magdalena." For a moment she admired the knife as though it was the most precious jewel in the world, then snapped from her admiration when she remembered why she'd come upstairs. "Where is The Hands?"

Mister Monoxide stepped out of the bedroom and pushed open the bathroom door. The Maitresse followed his gesture to see Maxine Elsworth squeezed into the bathtub under running cold water. Naked from the waist up, her skin was cracked and as black as tar, whilst her eyes were blind and milky.

The Maitresse rushed to her side. "Oh, Maxine. I will torture him for what he has done to you."

The Hands rolled her blind eyes around the room. "Get him to The Secretary. The One True Lord is with me. He has gifted me additional life that you may finish our mission. Go now whilst I have time."

Mister Monoxide rested his hands on the shoulders of The Maitresse and eased her up. "We'll come back for you, Maxine. We'll deliver the Son of Light and come straight back for you. Stay alive, then by this evening you shall dine in hell beside The Prince himself."

----- X -----

In the hallway, Merry Murder picked up the devil mask and bowler hat. He wanted them. He wanted a souvenir, a reminder of the time he fought an angel and won. He put the hat on his own head and looped his arm through the fixing straps of the mask. "How do we lift him?"

Mister Monoxide was coming down the staircase with The Maitresse. Sentinel asked, "Professor, could you get one end and lift it to your shoulder? I'll lift the middle. Doctor, please lift the other end to your shoulder."

It was awkward, trying to lift a heavy man taped to a pole. He was groggy but not totally out of it and he squirmed in slow but powerful undulations, like a worm trying to free itself from a fishing hook. They looked like urban hunters with a big game kill. Mister Monoxide led the way, shuffling with one end of the pole over his shoulder as he navigated the kitchen. At the other end, Merry Murder had the pole across his shoulder and between them, Mister Deathmask hung suspended, his arms cuffed around the pole, his ankles, knees and neck taped. Sentinel used her gifted strength to wrap an arm underneath the Son of Light and lift him to ease the weight. Despite her slight frame, she could probably lift double what the men could.

Once outside The Maitresse led the way, clutching the knife in her right hand. They threaded through the garden entrance and went to the van.

Sentinel opened the doors then helped them bundle their victim inside.

A voice came from behind them. Youthful. "What you doin', why has you got that man, yeah?"

Mister Monoxide heard The Maitresse replying. "It's not a real man, Dear. It's a mannequin for a clothing store."

"Nah! No way, he is moving, I can see him moving."

The Maitresse laughed. "Not at all, Dear. Come closer, take a look."

In the van, Mister Monoxide pulled the Son of Light inside. It was difficult, he had to pull from a stooped position, he was sweating and feeling breathless. From outside of the van, Sentinel and Merry Murder pushed the pole as Monoxide pulled. Merry Murder gave a thumbs-up when they had him deep enough inside.

Mister Monoxide climbed out of the van wheezing from exertion. Sentinel called to The Maitresse and said, "I'll ride with the Son of Light and the men. If this guy gives any trouble I want to be there. Can you take my car alone?"

"Yes, of course. I think we should leave quickly."

Mister Monoxide took a deep breath of fresh air then used his poison mask for a narcotic hit. "Maitresse?" he asked. "Were you talking with somebody?"

The Maitresse didn't answer verbally but directed his attention to a young, black boy, slumped against a garden wall. The kid's head was rocked to the side and his neck was spurting blood. The Maitresse held up the Eye of Magdalena and whispered, "This is a very powerful thing, Professor."

CHAPTER TEN

Sentinel dragged the front end of the pole down the steps of Almassy House. Across her shoulder was Mister Deathmask's brass canister of flammable liquid and in her pockets his brass knuckles. Navigating the tight passageway was difficult. With each step, the far end of the pole scraped and dropped with a thud, step by step, descending deeper under London. The Maitresse Bathory led the way, her head held high, the Eye of Magdalena clutched in her right hand. Sentinel appeared to be imbued with a new physical strength; the son of light was heavy, but Sentinel was sure on her feet and strong in her arms. She had him. She had the man who had killed The Pain. The man who had tried to kill Merry Murder. The man responsible for leaving The Hands mortally wounded in a bathtub. He would have killed them all.

Not now.

Sentinel pulled him into the cavern, then Mister Monoxide and Merry Murder took over, lifting the ends of the pole and taking him to the fire pit whilst he squirmed on the skewer. The duct tape around his head and neck rendered him mute and the tightness around his throat made his yellowed eyes bulge.

Sentinel laid out the souvenirs on the table; the pressurised brass canister of petrol, the knuckledusters. Merry Murder placed the mask and bowler hat beside them, arranging the objects into an exhibit. "We should get a display cabinet," he said.

The Maitresse swished the ornate knife through the air like a conductor with a baton. "I trust you have enough coal, Professor?"

"We have the coals. The Secretary will be with us shortly." He joined her to look at the knife. "You were right. It is a beautiful thing."

For a moment, it looked as though she had a tear in her eye. In a whisper, she said, "It speaks to me. I can sense it. The One True Lord is telling me to protect it and keep it safe." She ran the tip of her little finger below her right eye. If there was a tear it was swiftly removed. "Oh, Professor, we are here at last."

Merry Murder unlocked the vestibule. The girl was blinking in the light. Luke was sitting upright with his back to the wall. There was a smell of vomit from the cell where the young doctor had thrown up on his shirt. "Hello, Nikki," he spoke with his seduction voice. "Come out and make yourself useful. Crawl over there. Crawl, with your ass in the air. Arouse me."

Dutifully, as though in a dream state, Nikki began crawling.

"What the hell are you doing?" Luke slurred. "I don't…" he gasped a few breaths trying to find the strength, "I don't know who the hell you are anymore."

Merry Murder put his hands on his hips. "You never knew who I was, Luke. You never knew how powerful I am. Nor did you know about the pleasures I take or the eternity I have ahead of me; but, you're about to become a first-hand witness." He called over his shoulder, "Mister Monoxide, I think your gas is wearing off on this one."

The Professor and The Maitresse joined Merry Murder to look down on the young doctor. "What shall we do with it?" The Maitresse said with an air of mischief.

"We should present them to The Secretary as conspirators," Mister Monoxide said. "She won't want them, but she may enjoy seeing the face of the enemy."

To Luke directly, The Maitresse asked, "What do you want, young man?" She pointed the Eye of Magdalena at him. "I know what I want from you. I had a husband once who was a very cruel man. He was a philanderer. He humiliated and shamed me at every turn, living for the pleasures of his own cock… until I cut it off him… And he looked just like you."

Mister Monoxide took his breathing mask and enjoyed a nice long draw before offering it to Luke. "Maybe you would like a little more of my special mixture before The Maitresse castrates you?"

"What do you want, Luke?" Merry Murder asked.

The young doctor spoke thinly. "I just want to go home."

The Maitresse rocked her head back and laughed. "I'll make you a deal. I'll let you live, but it's either without your cock or without your balls. Which will you live without?"

Luke began slowly getting to his feet, sliding up the wall. "Please," he whispered. His eyes closed tightly as he fought for the strength but he looked ready to collapse.

"Ha ha ha, no I'm just kidding. I'm cutting it all off, then I'm killing you."

"No, you can't… I just… I just want…" then he darted forward, slamming his shoulder into The Maitresse, knocking her onto her ass. He ran drunkenly but firmly, shocking his tormentors. It was a ruse, he was fitter and stronger than he appeared. His hands were cuffed behind his back and Merry Murder almost got his hands around them, his fingers skimmed the chain between the manacles.

Mister Monoxide called for their soldier. "Sentinel!"

Within a second she drew the target pistol and let off a shot that shattered the young doctor's right heel bone. It happened as his foot left the ground. He was running. He had momentum carrying him forward when the small hole popped in the shoe leather. As it touched the floor the shattered bone fragments crunched through nerves and flesh, bringing him down with a scream.

Mister Monoxide helped The Maitresse back to her feet. "My dear, are you hurt?"

"No, I think I'm fine. The little bastard just shocked me."

Luke was on his front, nose and lips bloody from

smashing his face into the floor. Sentinel approached and trained the gun on the back of his right knee… Bang… Luke screamed. The .22 ammo wasn't guaranteed to kneecap somebody through the front, the patella is tough against small ammunition, but shooting through the back of the knee caused irreparable damage to the soft tissues. "You're going nowhere, fucker."

Luke grit his teeth to try and tough-out the pain, but all he wanted to do was scream.

Merry Murder moved to Luke and squat on his haunches. "Luke, you're not leaving this place alive. But if it's any consolation, before you die, you'll see something ordinary people are never privileged enough to see. You're about to meet Satan's Secretary." Merry Murder gave a wide grin. "My goodness, you're in for a treat."

Luke stared back with a look of incredulity, the pain from his leg so shocking it almost blurred everything else out. "What the fuck are you talking about?"

----- X -----

Nikki opened another charcoal bag and poured the contents into the pit. She was on her knees, spreading the briquettes with her hands. Luke was slumped by the edge of the pit, his hands still cuffed, blood pooling from the small bullet holes through the back of his knee and heel. He was looking at Mister Deathmask tied to a pole.

"Do you know who that is?" Merry Murder asked.

"I don't care," Luke whispered back.

"He's a hybrid, a cross between a human and an angel. His body is human."

"An angel… sure." Nothing surprised anymore.

"I know. He stinks of shit and looks like a tramp, but I assure you that is what he is."

"And what are you?"

Merry Murder paused for a moment, he bit his bottom lip with a half-scowl, contemplating his answer. "What am I? I'm blessed, that's what I am. I was chosen to be super fucking special. Each of us here is blessed. We've each given our earthly lives to the One True Lord in exchange for an eternity of bliss. We are very special people, Luke, very special. Billions of people have prayed to one God or another, but only a handful are ever offered an afterlife."

Luke looked down to his shattered leg. Blood was seeping out of his shoe and his trousers felt warm and wet, but it didn't hurt so long as he kept it dead still. "Whatever, man."

"No, this is true. What I'm telling you is totally true. Each of us; myself, Sentinel, Mister Monoxide and The Maitresse were singled out by the One True Lord. Take The Maitresse over there. She murdered her husband in the most gruesome fashion. He deserved it, the man was a horror. He would beat that lovely lady and rape her, he would keep her tormented and terrified; but not just her, he would beat and rape other women too. Finally, she just snapped and cut off her husband's balls with a pair of kitchen scissors. She enjoyed it so much she became obsessed with castration fantasies. She would cut the dicks off everything from rabbits to horses. The One True Lord loved that; and that's when he touched her. He made her so she could enjoy her fetish as much as she wished. All he asked is that she serve him."

"And what about you?" Luke barely had any volume to his voice. "Are you cutting off dicks, too?"

"Ha. No, I like watching women die. I like when they have no escape. I like being a doctor and administering drugs to pretty, young things who place their trust in me. And, I love it most of all when they're at their emotional end. I love the desperate. I love the lost and needy who throw themselves at the feet of a saviour, especially when the saviour offers nothing but misery." He tipped his head towards Nikki. "Like sugar-tits over there."

Luke turned his head away. "You're insane... Jesus, this is..."

"...Never mention the 'J' word. That guy was a fucking tool."

"Look, Doctor Hill, what do you think you're going to get out of this? Surely you don't believe you're going to get life after death, do you? There is no God. There's no such thing as angels. It's not true."

Merry Murder laughed and pointed to the circle of charcoal briquettes. "In a few minutes, Satan's Secretary is going to rise out of the fire right there, right before your very fucking eyes. You're going to see just how true it all is. She's going to take the Son of Light with her back to hell and torment him forever. You'll be less lucky. There's no afterlife for you. There's nothing for you. When you're dead, you're dead. It won't take long."

----- X -----

"Nikki, come back over here and kneel next to Luke."

She dutifully obeyed but as she stared at the blood surrounding Luke's foot she drifted back from the hypnosis of Merry Murder's voice. "Oh, God," she whispered. She glanced across her shoulder to see Sentinel hovering behind. Mister Monoxide was breathing through his plastic mask as he walked atop the coals, squeezing out fire-lighting fluid.

"Are you okay?" Luke whispered. She made a slight nod and swallowed hard. She looked to the blood that surrounded Luke. "I'm alright. I'm injured, but I'm okay." Very quietly he whispered, "Can you run if you need to?"

Nikki mouthed the word, "Maybe."

"I can't move, so if a chance to escape appears, I want you to run to the stairs. I'll try and stop them or slow them down, but I want you to get to those stairs, get to the top and scream for help. Understand?"

"Where is the blood coming from?"

"My foot and my knee. The black woman shot me."

Nikki gasped. "Does it hurt?"

"It's numb. Look, the first chance you see, you've got to make a break for it, I'll do something. I'll block their path or interfere, but you've…"

…Whoosh! Flames leapt up as Mister Monoxide threw a match onto the pit. The Maitresse walked the fire holding the ornate knife. "Look at you two," she said. "Like lovers, talking in whispers. Are you conspiring? Are you making plans to escape?" Nikki held her gaze but noticed Luke lowered his, betraying his intentions. "It won't work you know." She called out louder, "Sentinel. I think this one is plotting to escape."

From behind, Sentinel said, "I'd like to see how fast he can escape on only one leg."

"No, the other one. The sow. The little bitch is thinking of running."

Sentinel looked at Nikki directly. "Is that a fact. Stand up, girl." Nikki didn't move. Sentinel pulled her gun from the holster. "I said stand up." Slowly at first, then with full commitment, Nikki got to her feet as the pistol was pointed at her. She turned her head to look at The Maitresse who was gleefully smiling. As Nikki returned her gaze to Sentinel the pistol kicked in her hand and Nikki was falling forward as though someone had just ripped the rug out from under her feet. Her chin hit the floor. Her hands were up to break the fall but she landed hard. Then came a blistering pain from her right foot that made her howl.

Mister Monoxide yelled, "Be quiet, girl," but she couldn't help herself.

"I'm afraid she won't be able to," The Maitresse said. "Sentinel has just hobbled her. They're now a matching pair of cripples." The Maitresse pointed her ornate knife at Nikki and said, "You won't leave this place alive, you cunt."

The pain pulsed up Nikki's leg like the nerves were electrified. The front of the ankle joint, where the top of her foot met the shin, had a clean bullet hole that had hit like a sledgehammer to shatter the talus. It had cracked open the bone and tore open every nerve. The lead slug was wedged deep inside. Nikki rolled to her side and pulled her knees to her chest to grab at the wound. She screamed for a moment then tried to grit her teeth to stop.

She saw something.

Everybody in the cave was looking at her.

They weren't looking at Mister Deathmask. If they had, they would have noticed the ghostly little girl moving between solid and smoke as she drifted around the handcuffs. Nikki screamed again, allowing the pain to help her become a distraction. Then she felt a surge of hope as the Son of Light's hands broke from their bindings.

----- X -----

The coals were glowing and the heat coming from them made the faces of the cultists shimmer. Sentinel was directly behind Nikki and Luke. To their left, Mr

Deathmask was lying in stillness against the pole.

The cultists focussed on the fire.

Nikki was looking for Magdalena, watching Mr Deathmask from the corner of her eye. "Please," she whispered. "Magdalena, if you're here, please help me."

To her surprise, the little girl's voice came back, whispered right in her ear. The little girl had only one instruction. "Kill yourself."

Then to the centre of the coals came movement, like something was beneath the surface, rippling the top layer.

"Hail to the One True Lord," Merry Murder called as he punched both hands in the air. "Hail to Him. Glory to the One True Lord."

The Maitresse joined in. "Praise Him in all of his majesty."

Through the shimmering heat waves, Nikki became fixated on Mister Monoxide. He was grinning, lit by the red fire, his face wobbled through the heated air. His wide grin revealing sharp little teeth.

Something moved in the centre of the pit, something rising. "Oh, my God." Nikki gasped. "What the fuck?"

Sentinel hit the gun butt into her temple. "Show reverence to The Secretary, sow."

From the pit, the motion grew stronger until Nikki saw the woman emerging from the coals.

"Hail to the One True Lord," Merry Murder called again.

The Maitresse dropped her head, allowing her chin to rest against her chest with her eyes tightly closed and her right hand in the air brandishing the knife… The knife… this time when Nikki saw it she felt a sensation like cold hands were turning her head to look at it. "Kill yourself," came Magdalena's voice again.

"Never," she whispered back.

"My Madam, My Master." Mister Monoxide held out both arms as though reaching to hug the emerging woman. "Command me and I shall throw myself at your service."

From the fire pit the head and shoulders of the woman had completely emerged, her head adorned with hot, golden jewellery. She rose higher to reveal heavy breasts with a golden chain between pierced nipples. Flakes of glowing ash and embers fell away from her shoulders. She rose higher, her pubic hair on fire with flames that licked the golden broach in her navel. Nikki heard Luke take a huge and slow intake of breath. His body was pulling back, his whole being trying to move away. Sentinel pressed the muzzle of her gun against the back of his head to keep him still. He began shaking uncontrollably.

"Hail to The Secretary," Merry Murder cried out. "May our efforts please her."

The emerging woman stepped up onto the coals and began walking the circle. She looked at each of the cultists one at a time but paused by Sentinel. "Is this our day? Is this the day we make love?"

"We have him." She pointed towards the chained Son of Light against the floor. Her voice lost its power as she spoke, weakened by emotion. "We have the Son of Light as you commanded."

Her voice growled as she bared her teeth in a grin. "And who are these?"

Nikki felt her stomach fall away as the demon looked into her eyes.

"They are his accomplices."

The Secretary looked between Nikki and Luke then held her hand only inches from Sentinel's face as though she wanted to touch her skin. She stared deeply, longingly, into her eyes. "And you have brought me the Son of Light."

"We have. We have brought him here for you."

The Secretary held her gaze for a moment longer then began her slow walk around the edge of the fire. "You will burn for eternity, Son of Light. You shall be made to worship a new master and your degradation shall be without limitation." Then to all of the cultists she said, "Bring him to me."

Mister Monoxide and Merry Murder took hold of either end of the pole. As they lifted him he somehow looked different. It was his legs, they weren't taped to the pole, rather they were wrapped around it. As they strained to lift him the Son of Light suddenly dropped his legs to stand on the floor, his arms quickly came free and grabbed the pole.

Nobody had a chance to say anything but in

Nikki's head she said one phrase, 'He's free.'

Mr Deathmask grabbed the pole and swung it hard and fast around his body. Above her, Nikki saw Sentinel point the gun. From nowhere, black smoke leapt into being, swirling instantly into the form of an eyeless little girl in a white dress; she moved like a spiral, grabbing the gun as she revolved around the weapon and pushed it down to one side by a ghostly vortex of force. The weapon discharged into the fire throwing up a shower of sparks.

The Secretary ran to the edge of the pit and reached out, trying to grab the Son of Light, but without stepping out of the fire. "Keep Him," she yelled. "Hold him." But the Son of Light was now on his feet, brandishing a steel pole which he smashed into the face of Merry Murder. The doctor dropped backwards, missing teeth, his nose pissing blood. He got up quickly and ran at Mr Deathmask who was swinging the pole towards Mister Monoxide. They grappled, but he had more strength than both cultists combined.

Mister Monoxide screamed, "Sentinel!" but she was still trying to aim her weapon around a rapidly moving black mist that pulled at her gun every time she aligned the sights.

Nikki saw her chance. She stood on her one good foot and began to hop. Then she saw another option. Magdalena read the situation and swung around Sentinel's head, her little hands covering the sharpshooter's eyes and pulling her backwards against

Luke. With hardly any leverage, Nikki jammed her shoulder into Sentinel's stomach and toppled her across Luke onto the fire pit. She screamed and shrieked as the heat burned her clothes. She tried to stand, screaming and wailing but her foot dropped straight through as deep as the knee as though the pit was much deeper than it had been.

For a full second, the ghostly form of Magdalena materialised before her as though to watch the woman sink deeper into the coals. "You will burn."

"Nooooo!" Sentinel screamed out, aiming her gun. She fired three times as her body sunk deeper, each bullet hitting Magdalena but passing through like a knife through cigarette smoke.

"YOU DISEASED CUNT!" The Secretary had her finger pointed to Magdalena and her words came out with a blast of heat.

Magdalena smirked. "Hello, Leonora."

The Secretary tensed her muscles and made her hands into fists. She closed her eyes and grit her teeth, straining under exertion. Her skin began to crack across her body showing a fire beneath the dermis. Flames spit between the cracks as a blowtorch-like, fierce blue flame shot from both her eyes. "You," she said. "I will take you instead."

Nikki tried to step on her injured foot but the blast of nerve pain hit like a shotgun that brought her crashing to the floor. As she went down The Maitresse ran past, heading for the exit. She would have made it too except

Magdalena vanished from above and rematerialized by The Maitresse to pull her hair. She spun the old woman and toppled her to the floor. The ornate knife falling from her grip. As The Maitresse got to her feet she looked to the knife on the floor and the ghostly little girl blocking it. She looked to see Mister Monoxide being pummelled by the Son of Light… and in panic… she ran for the staircase.

By the side of the pit, Mister Deathmask pounded his fists into the face of Mister Monoxide. He'd gotten the old man on his back and was straddling the professor, laying powerful punches into his face whilst Merry Murder tried to pull him off. Deathmask fought like a tiger against two sheep.

A great bellowing noise came forth as The Secretary screamed. Her skin darkened to something like burned leather and her golden jewellery brightened to white hot. By her feet, Sentinel had sunk to her waist in the coals. She held the back of her left hand against her face as though trying to shield the heat. Her screams were like fingernails on a blackboard. Suddenly she found her wherewithal and pointed the gun, still in her possession, towards Deathmask. The Son of Light recognised the danger and in a split second dragged Merry Murder across him as a shield. Sentinel let out a shot that hit directly between Merry Murder's shoulder blades. Then Deathmask stood, lifted the doctor almost above his head and threw him at Sentinel. The Secretary got there first, reaching out with growing hands that were starting to show talons. She managed to block the doctor and push him away so he didn't fall completely into the pit. He landed face down and unmoving, his shins and feet overhanging the pit and against the coals.

Sentinel tried to aim again but as she did, her body suddenly dropped to her armpits and the shot went high of its mark. Her hair erupted into flames. "No," she cried out. "My Lord, I'm sorry," with that, she was sucked screaming beneath the fire.

Nikki began crawling towards the exit. With each movement, the bones in her foot crunched with a nerve pain that would have been insurmountable had she not been so desperate and jacked on adrenaline. She saw the black mist of Magdalena shoot past her, hugging the floor, rushing towards something that glistened in the light. A hand came out of the mist and grabbed the object then rushed it back to her. For a single second Magdalena appeared in full form as it handed her the knife. "Kill yourself. You must." Then she vanished. Nikki took the knife and continued crawling, commando style, pulling forward on her forearms with her belly on the floor.

With Mister Monoxide barely able to roll over and Merry Murder's feet roasting on the fire pit, Mister Deathmask went to the table and took his fuel can, mask and hat. Magdalena appeared to Mister Deathmask in full form. "Get away from here," she said. "Kill the old woman. I'll kill Leonora."

As he ran to the exit, Nikki saw him pressing his fingers into the brass knuckles. "Don't leave me," she whispered. "Please, God, don't abandon me." He looked to her briefly as he pulled on the mask, then he vanished into the staircase.

"Please," Nikki cried futilely. "Please, help me."

She was abandoned. She had the Eye of Magdalena.

Over her shoulder, Nikki could see Mister Monoxide getting to his knees. She saw Luke crawling away from the fire pit at a snail's pace. She saw The Secretary, now part transformed into something hideous. Sharp shoulder blades jutting from her back. Her face seemed to be pulling forward like the snout of a dog. It was still human looking, but less so than it had been.

Nikki continued crawling until she heard Luke screaming in a worse and more shrill sound than she had ever heard. Mister Monoxide was dragging Luke by his hair to the fire pit. The Secretary walking atop the flames was now more animal than human and the hideous thing reached to grab Luke with a single hand that wrapped around his head. With unimaginable strength, she lifted him with one hand and Nikki watched in horror as his clothes burst into flames and his body jerked in the fire. Like a twitching corpse in the hangman's noose, Luke jerked and writhed as he burned, held in the clenched fist of a demon.

Nikki crawled another few feet and felt Magdalena beside her. "Kill yourself and you will be immortal. But if they kill you, they'll torment you for eternity."

"Never!" She pulled herself forward, looking at the

knife in her hand. The exit looked so far away. She looked back across her shoulder and watched as The Secretary tossed Luke's flaming corpse to her side. Then the worst thing she could imagine happened. The Secretary stepped out of the fire pit. The naked woman pressed one foot onto the cold ground and shrieked as though she'd stepped onto broken glass. Another foot came out and again she screamed in agony as her body fell forward on to her hands and knees. Life outside the fire-pit was as painful for her as the burning coals would be to anybody else. But now her haunches elongated, her legs bending like a dog. She was out of the fire and was transforming to look more ghoulish and monstrous; her form was still that of a woman, but now she exuded a sickening revulsion rather than sexuality. She was in silhouette save for the fire glow cast around the cavern and her shape was beastly. Beside her, limped Mister Monoxide, wounded but still her devoted minion. The Secretary began to stand, acclimatising to the cold Earth beyond the fire.

Nikki crawled harder, faster, but from behind she could almost feel the breath of The Secretary burning through her clothes as her anger breathed on her like the snorts of a dragon. She wouldn't look behind. She would keep crawling, keep trying to get to the exit.

Her ankle was grabbed.

She was pulled backwards.

It was like a branding iron had gripped her. She screamed but no noise came out. She didn't have to look back to know it was The Secretary. With one of her burning hands holding onto her, the demon was dragging her to the fire pit, she would burn her alive.

"Please. No," she cried softly, "I won't." With the remainder of her strength she jerked her body, pulling her legs to her chest, or rather pulling her chest down to meet her knees.

Magdalena's voice came back one more time. "Now. Do it now or they'll own you forever."

Nikki tucked in tightly and squealed as she did so. She felt Mister Monoxide pulling at her, gripping her hair to stretch her out, a small silver pistol in his hand. She barely had the strength to resist. Then she felt the world cascading through colours and emotions, twinkling lights of a billion prisms flashing rainbows in the dark and at the same time saw Mister Monoxide pointing his small silver revolver at her. She saw the muzzle flash three times but didn't feel the bullets hit.

For a moment there was nothing.

Then the world faded back in with the sight of Mister Monoxide leaning across her as the monstrous Secretary stretched out her arms. With the very last of her strength she tilted her eyes down to see the Eye of Magdalena, wedged to the hilt below her ribcage. Mister Monoxide grabbed it and pulled it out and the world went black.

Magdalena spoke in the darkness. "Well done. Now we can be one."

CHAPTER ELEVEN

The Maitresse Bathory made it to the top of the stairs, panting for breath. Too many stairs. Too rich an age to do it quickly. She ran through the office and into the corridor of Almassy House. A night security man at the reception said, "Good night," then noticing her distress asked, "are you alright?"

The Maitresse wanted to say something, she wanted help to get away. It was all going wrong. She had to escape, but where could she go? Would the One True Lord punish her for cowardice? Yes. He would revoke his invitation. She was wrong to do this. She was wrong about everything and she was panicking. She glanced back across her shoulder and saw the Son of Light come out of the office. "Stop this man!" she shrieked to the guard. "Help me. He wants to kill me."

She ran.

The guard was young and fit; he saw the devil mask coming. "Hold it." He tried to get in the way but was pushed back. The guard tried again and lunged low to wrap his arms around Deathmask's waist, trying to down him with a rugby tackle.

It delayed him by seconds but it was enough. The Maitresse got onto High Holborn. People were in the streets by the Underground station. Yes. Get to the station. She could lose herself in the crowd. She chanced a quick glance back over her shoulder and saw the Son of Light still wrestling with the guard.

In the cavern, Nikki felt as though she was floating. One of her eyes opened slightly but didn't move or focus. The world was sideways, like shot from a TV camera that had fallen on its side.

The Secretary looked like a haggard woman. Her golden jewellery dimmed to tarnished brass, her lustrous skin now worn leather, her high cheekbones had become sagging jowls. Mister Monoxide was limping, his right knee causing him trouble. He brought his black overcoat and held it whilst the haggard old Secretary slipped her arms in. "The Son of Light," she said, "is still within our grasp. Help me capture him alive and your place amongst the legends is assured."

Mister Monoxide began fastening his coat over The Secretary like a parent buttoning up the coat of a child. "He is too strong for me alone," he said.

"I have seen. I will take him. You will help me."

Mister Monoxide motioned towards the staircase. "I will give everything I have for you."

Through her sideways vision, Nikki watched them leave.

Her eyesight faded into darkness until the voice of

Magdalena came again. "You may stand now, my friend."

In her mind, Nikki said the words, "I can't."

"You can. Let me move you."

For a moment, Nikki's vision returned and the scene began rolling upright, turning itself as her brain began to see the world as it should be. But then she recognised it wasn't her brain that was moving, it was her body. She was moving upright without any kind of effort. "What is happening?"

"We are one," Magdalena said. "We have made the handshake of light and we are together. Step forward."

Nikki tried, her injured foot scraping the floor but not hurting. As she looked down it almost appeared as though her foot turned to smoke as she shuffled and only fully materialised as it put pressure on the floor. "Oh, my God. What is happening?"

----- X -----

The Maitresse pressed between couples holding hands, she crashed against a woman leaving a coffee shop and tipped the drink across her coat. "Hey. Careful."

The Maitresse didn't stop. She could see the entrance to the Underground station and chanced a quick glance back to see Deathmask with his devil mask and bowler hat running towards her. He swept his arms through the crowd. He pushed away couples like they were toddlers, he knocked back the woman cleaning the coffee from her coat.

"NOOOO! Help, help me!" The Maitresse cried out in a panic. By sheer luck, a taxi pulled up alongside, its yellow sign saying it was ready for business. The Maitresse grabbed at the handle and practically threw herself inside. "Please. Get me away from here." But it was too late. As she climbed to the back seat, Deathmask pulled her out and pushed her against the bodywork before landing a huge smashing punch to her head. Brass knuckles in full effect, the skin tore and the osteoporosis of old age crumbled her jawbone. Another swing, this time from the left, the brass knuckles hit the side of her head and cleaved her right ear right down the middle.

Another punch, another, another, another. The world blurred and flashed for the old lady as she felt herself sliding down under the barrage of hits.

For a moment it stopped and she caught sight of two big men trying to restrain the Son of Light. The ordinary people of London would never stand idle as an old woman was assaulted in the street.

She was bloody, she was disoriented but somehow climbed into the back of the cab and pulled the door closed. "Help me! Please!"

The cab driver gunned the engine and the car began to move as the Son of Light threw off the mortals trying to make their citizen's arrest. He swung a punch at the window and shattered the glass, hooking his arm through to hold the vehicle as it tried to speed away. He clung to the outside but got a hand to the front offside door handle as his feet dragged on the road. He opened the door and managed to raise a leg and press it forward, catching a foothold. His right arm was hooked through the broken window, his left foot was inside the door. In the back of the cab, The Maitresse screamed to the sky as the cab driver tried to kick at the Son of Light's leg. Within seconds, Mister Deathmask had the advantage and was climbing into the front with the driver. They scuffled. The vehicle ploughed into a woman crossing the street, throwing her across the car, then careened into the barriers surrounding a crossroads.

The Son of Light smashed against the dashboard, the driver cracked his ribs on the steering wheel; and in the back The Maitresse was thrown forward to smash her face against the glass screen that separates driver and client.

Deathmask looked back at her through the bloody screen. The driver opened his door and fell out onto the road holding his stomach. More of London's helpful citizens ran to assist, but it was too late for The Maitresse. She was going nowhere.

----- X -----

In the caverns, Nikki glided towards the fire pit and saw the slowly burning body of Doctor Luke Edwards, half sunken into the coals. He looked more like a shop mannequin, charred black, with all the detail removed from his face as the subcutaneous fat bubbled through the cracks in his skin.

Not caring for the heat, Nikki reached out her right hand feeling it unnaturally heavy. She grasped Luke's leg and pulled him from the pit, lifting his body into her arms. His blackened head hung loose and his arms drooped lifeless.

There was a strange pull in Nikki. Part of her wanted to go and take part in some other enterprise whilst her more rational self wanted to take in the image of the murdered young doctor.

"What am I feeling?" she whispered to herself.

"Take a moment," Magdalena said. "We both must come to terms with how we share the vessel."

Almost immediately, Nikki understood, with detail and to the end of its intricate ramifications. "You're in here with me, aren't you?"

"We're in here together; and soon we will become a single, unified whole."

----- X -----

The Secretary and Mister Monoxide made it to the entranceway of Almassy House. "Did you see which way the big man went?"

The guard at the desk was nursing a bloody nose. "Do you know him? I've called the police."

"Where is he?" The Secretary cackled her words like a Walt Disney witch. The guard pointed to the big glass doorway.

Mister Monoxide led the way, holding the door

open for The Secretary and seeing immediately a commotion further along the street. Traffic was stopped. It looked like an accident on the junction.

----- X -----

Nikki was transported into the memories of Magdalena. She was in a church, buried underground. The sensation was beyond any experience she had ever known. New memories were gifted that, once seen, felt as old as time itself. She was in a domed room with classical paintings on the curved walls. Paintings of filth and degradation; oil paintings of tortures and impalements, of skin being flayed, of men being burned and children being skewered. There was a painting of a man gleefully eating shit, whilst another showed an old woman eating the testicles of young boys like they were olives.

"Where am I?"

"This is where The Secretary made me. In her church."

Nikki remembered it all. Twelve children wearing cotton baptism gowns. They were tied to twelve chairs arranged in a circle. The domed room was filled with their crying as a man with blonde hair and clothes from another century, spoke in an unknown language. He brought a circular platter of twelve knives, their tips touching, their handles adorned with ruby gemstones.

A woman was there, a young and beautiful woman with dusky skin, something about her made Nikki think of Roma gypsies. It was The Secretary. Her features were different, more human. In this form, she was an ordinary person, not the demon who had risen from the fire or the old hag who had stepped out of the flames.

The gypsy took hold of a knife. A phrase flashed through her mind of another melded memory. "The Twelve of Darkness," she whispered. "Magdalena is one of The Twelve of Darkness."

The knife blade came to her face.

"Stop. Are you crazy? STOP!"

But nothing can stop a memory of such pain. In Magdalena's case, not even being dead for hundreds of years would stop the memory of having her eyes cut out.

----- X -----

The taxi engine was hissing steam from its ruptured radiator. More Londoners had come to help the driver; they had him laid out to administer first aid. "Watch out he's a fucking madman," somebody shouted. "The guy in the mask is a fucking madman."

"There's a woman in the back," a girl shouted tugging at the door. The impact had bent the chassis and the door frame was buckled and jammed.

"Are you alright mate?" A hand came in to help the Son of Light as he climbed out of the cab.

"The guy in the mask is a maniac," a voice warned. "Stay away from him."

Deathmask saw people tugging at the back door

and saw The Maitresse inside with a bloody face. His sense of purpose returned along with his determination. The people were tugging at the door. A big man was needed. A man with strength. Mister Deathmask pushed the helpful aside, grabbed at the door and pulled it so hard he could have torn off the hinges. He bent the metal back and went for the brass canister hung across his shoulder.

"You've got to watch out for this guy. He's crazy. Grab him, grab his arms."

He found the trigger mechanism at the end of the hose. He sprayed, the fuel hissing out and splattering the car interior, soaking into the clothing of The Maitresse. Then he was being pulled back, sprayed fuel hitting some of his assailants. One man with a thick beard tried to tackle him lower, grabbing about the knees to pull from the legs but the Son of Light was firmly rooted. Beard-man's eyes widened as he saw the flame come to life. He had fuel on himself. They all did.

The first fireball went up with a growled 'whooff', it was outside the car and sent the attackers darting to the side. By now the mobile phone cameras were recording and for one young woman, she captured the perfect shot of Mister Deathmask standing in a fireball with four other men diving away from him.

Then the second fireball went up from inside the taxi cab. There was screaming and scrambling inside as The Maitresse was engulfed in flames. She rushed for the door and found only the boot of Mister Deathmask hitting square in the chest to kick her back into the furnace.

Deathmask himself was on fire, his coat and sleeve were ablaze and he patted the flames down as he walked from the burning car. Around him, the four assailants were on fire to varying degrees and had either run like crazy or dropped and rolled. The man with the beard had been engulfed; he dropped and didn't move. Flames were coming from his back but nobody was helping him.

There was a loud bang to his left side.

The second bang went off in the side of his leg just above the knee and dropped him to the floor. He had a moment to hear screams and see the helpful Londoners switch into a mode of self-preservation and panic.

Mister Monoxide was closing in with the little snub nose revolver hot in his fist whilst The Secretary shuffled along behind him.

----- X -----

Memories were streaming into Nikki's mind. She was a little girl bridesmaid on the green hillside of a rolling valley, a chain of flowers on her head. She could even smell the countryside. It was the happiest memory of Magdalena.

She snapped back to her real surroundings. The pain in her foot was gone. "What has passed?" she whispered. "Where is my body?"

As she moved, her legs seemed to vanish into

smoke and with the first few steps she seemed to find a memory of movement. Instinct, or some other deeper knowledge. She was moving as mist. In her head, she heard the whisper of Magdalena as she said, "We are as I am."

Mister Deathmask. He was in trouble. She could sense his pain.

Nikki didn't know quite how it happened but her body drifted lower and moved at speed, hugging the floor and rushing towards the exit. She found the staircase and ascended without ever placing a foot onto the stonework. She was a body of dark mist that glided only inches from the ground. "We must protect him."

----- X -----

Mister Deathmask was against the road, his right leg ruined. The bullet had gone in through the right side of his knee and blasted through the ligaments, tendons and nerves. He ripped away his mask to scream out with the pain. So close. So close to ending them all.

Mister Monoxide approached him cautiously with the gun in his outstretched arm. His teeth were gritted and his lips peeled back. His eyes momentarily moved to the flames coming from the taxi. In the back he could see the blackened shape of a woman surrounded by fire. Above the taxi came a thick and acrid plume of smoke. His eyes turned back to the woman in the cab. "Maitresse?" he whispered. "Oh, no… Maitresse… My

Maitresse." To Mister Deathmask he hissed the words, "You mother fucker!"

Deathmask could hear the first sirens approaching; and he could see the twisted form of The Secretary shuffling slowly towards him. "You will come with me," she hissed. "I will take you to your new master."

Then the first blue flashing light came into view, a police car rushing at them. A policeman and policewoman got out.

Mister Monoxide took aim with the pistol and fired one shot at the policeman, the bullet straying far to the side and ricocheting off the bonnet of the vehicle to crack the windscreen. It was enough to send the officers scurrying. The policewoman seemed to have her wits about her. She ran behind the car, grabbing the radio against her shoulder as she went for cover. The policeman sprinted to the underground station and dove through the front entrance. Mister Monoxide knew the next police to arrive would be able to shoot back. "There will be more," he said to The Secretary. "We don't have much time."

"Time enough," she hissed.

Together they approached the wounded Son of Light who, whilst trying to right himself to a sitting position managed to throw wild swinging punches until The Secretary laid her hands on him. "You are mine."

The Son of Light howled and screamed in agony, as though the very touch of The Secretary contained the venom of a thousand vipers. He fell back screaming as she took hold of his left foot and began dragging him along the road with a strength that seemed unnatural. She looked like an old woman dragging a blanket behind her rather than a heavyset giant of a man. Despite the Son of Light's screaming and flailing of his arms, he seemed powerless in her grip.

Sirens could be heard. They were only a few hundred yards to Almassy House. A few minutes to take him down the stairs and the Son of Light would be on the fire. The Secretary continued her shuffling walk but said to Mister Monoxide, "You have done well to bring me this far. Defend me. Ensure I succeed and your rightful reward of Kingdom shall be granted. Stay here, protect me."

Mister Monoxide stopped walking and checked his revolver. The Secretary only needed a few minutes to take the Son of Light to the fire pit, all he had to do was distract the police for a few minutes; and of course, stay alive. Once the Son of Light was taken, death meant nothing.

All he needed was a few minutes.

----- X -----

Nikki flew up the stairs like she was running on mist, her point of view was closer to the ground, like she was looking through the eyes of a small animal. For a moment she had a vision of herself like some kind of Chinese dragon that hugged the ground and moved in rapid beats of its tail, like a salamander that floated on air.

As she made it to the Almassy office she felt a sudden swelling of power as she flew to the door, smashing against it like a cannonball, cracking the woodwork. There was so much power and momentum behind the action that it made her scream with fright. There was real strength to her ethereal form.

As she reached out her right hand she realised she was holding a short cylinder of gold and silver, intricately detailed with a gemstone on one end. It seemed like it was glued to her hand; if not glued then she had to learn how to let go of it.

With her left hand she reached for the door handle and part grasped and part passed through it. It was anger inducing. Maddening. Why couldn't she control her body. "Let me do it!" Nikki said. "Let me do it."

Instantly the balance of power shifted and her form became more solid and human, her hand gripped the handle and turned it. Her feet were still misty and didn't fully connect to the floor.

In the lobby she discovered a security guard nursing a bloody nose. He was pressed against the big glass window of the lobby, watching something in the street. He heard her approach and turned around, suddenly throwing himself back against the glass with a look of utter horror on his face. "WHAT THE… WHAT THE…" Beyond the security guard, out in the street, Nikki could see the old hag dragging Mister Deathmask towards them. Magdalena took over and rushed them towards the great glass window. In that instant Nikki saw her reflection.

The security guard found his voice. "WHAT THE FUCK?"

Her reflection was little more than a glowing, ghostly woman, but she had powerful black feathered wings. As she rushed at the glass, her body curled to shoulder the impact and the wings drew in around her. She felt the glass shatter as surely as it had been blasted with a shotgun. Her body became a partial mist as she rolled across the ground. Splintered glass was falling around her. She rolled to her feet and opened her wings to their full eighteen feet width and swung forward with the cylinder in her right hand that was stretching out to become a sword.

The Secretary moved lightning fast and hit the blade away with her palm, but it cut her. The edge of the blade had cut across her fingers and she dropped Mister Deathmask to hold her injury.

Further down the street Mister Monoxide began running back to his master, his little silver revolver pointing the way as he sprinted as fast as his old body could move.

Magdalena controlled Nikki and swung the sword again, this time The Secretary ducked and evaded the attack. She smiled when she did it.

By her feet, Mister Deathmask stirred, free of her grip. He couldn't help; he couldn't even touch her without losing his strength, but he still had his can of fuel and began pulling it to the ready as Mister Monoxide rushed in. He sprayed the petrol, or what was left of it at Monoxide but got just as much on himself.

Beside them, Magdalena controlled Nikki's new body with wild swings of the sword, but The Secretary was too fast, too controlled. It was as though she could predict where the sword was aimed before it was ever swung.

Behind The Secretary, Mister Monoxide aimed his pistol at Nikki and fired a single shot. Instead of a splash of blood, there was a puff of black smoke. Mister Deathmask was trying to get to his feet. Monoxide screamed, "Get away from her," as he ran close. He fired another bullet into his foe, wounding the edge of his shoulder. Monoxide threw himself across him, trying to put his weight across Deathmask's chest. Then the gun went off in his hand. He didn't know how, but the gun fired and the heat from the barrel ignited the fuel and sent them both into an inferno. "Noooo!"

Nikki tried to relax her involvement. Magdalena was the better swordswoman, or at least the part of her where Magdalena resided was better, but as she swung and sliced through the air she missed again and again until the fireball went up behind The Secretary. Mister Monoxide was atop the Son of Light but they both went up in flames. Nikki recoiled and panicked, giving The Secretary a moment of advantage. A split-second error. In an instant, The Secretary had Nikki's sword hand gripped by the wrist and clasped her other hand to

Nikki's throat. The physical contact sucking the life out of her, stealing her momentum and movements. It locked her in a vulnerable position. "If I can't have your Son of Light," The Secretary hissed. "I'll take you instead." The power of The Secretary was undeniable, it was as though she was bleeding Nikki of all her strength, sapping her life force and choking her out of existence. Her legs became more solid and Nikki felt the cold of the road as her bare feet pressed against it. She felt the chill of the night air against her body and found her misty form was giving way to her weakened, naked self. The black smoke that had made her was blowing away to reveal the weak young girl within. "I will take you to Hell," The Secretary said. "I will own you. Your endless rapes of fire and suffering will become legend." Nikki's knees buckled under the loss of strength, her body turned more human and she felt the knife wound to her chest as she began to die for the second time. "The Prince shall devise new humiliations for you. New degradations. You shall be owned by the Prince and for eternity you will eat his shit on your hands and knees."

From behind The Secretary, Nikki saw flames rising, the man was standing, Mister Deathmask was getting to his feet. He was so cloaked in flames he was barely recognisable, but as he tried to stand on his one good leg Nikki felt a sudden burst of emotion. The memory flashed through her head of the subterranean church. She remembered The Secretary in her human form, clutching a knife that would come to be known as the Eye of Magdalena; and as she remembered the gypsy woman leaning in to blind her, she recalled the smirk and glowing excitement across her face.

"NEVER!" Nikki yelled.

At the same time, Mister Deathmask threw his flaming arms around The Secretary's neck and yanked her backwards. As her hands left Nikki's skin she felt a surge of power so unimaginably strong it almost burst from her. She leapt high, not to her feet, but higher still, her body aglow with light as her entire wingspan of black feathers unfurled about her, the golden sword shining with unimaginable light as she swung it around her head and sliced it down with the force of the ocean.

In the instant before connecting time slowed.

Just for a moment.

Time enough for the Son of Light to speak in her mind. "Goodbye, my love."

The sword connected.

Two heads were thrown into the air. The Secretary and Mister Deathmask met their end on the same strike.

----- X -----

Mister Monoxide stopped trying to pat down the flames. He stopped struggling as the pain subsided. The burns were so deep they had killed the nerves. He saw the burning decapitated body of The Secretary. "Oh, fuck." Then he died. His body was sitting upright, on fire, with the revolver in his hand.

----- X -----

The action had ended in the streets of Holborn, but the blue flashing lights and sirens were getting closer. Nikki held out her hands and looked at them. They were white, ethereal, milky in colour and almost made of light. "What are we?" she asked.

"We are together," Magdalena replied.

With that, Nikki allowed Magdalena to take control and carry them into the air. Her wings beat only twice before dissolving into mist and floating high across London. They followed the river East for a few minutes until Nikki felt compelled to turn their ghost flight to the North. "Here," she said pointing to an area far ahead. "I want to go here."

As silently as when she had taken off, the amalgamated form of Nikki and Magdalena landed in the centre of Abney Park cemetery. In her ghostly form, Nikki stepped between the crooked and damaged gravestones. "These are the dead," she whispered. "I think I can hear them."

"Maybe you can," Magdalena said. "Maybe it is a gift. We have made the handshake and been given a gift of eternal life."

Nikki floated between graves. She stretched out her wings for a moment then curled them to wrap around her body. "A gift from who?" The question was met with silence. "A gift from who?" she asked again. "Is it from God?"

"I don't think there is a God," Magdalena said. "There is something far more terrible."

Nikki took a seat on the edge of a grave and curled the wings around her. "So, what do we do now?"

"I don't know," Magdalena whispered. "I've dreamed of vengeance for centuries. But now that I've tasted it, I don't know what we're to do."

"We shall think of something," Nikki whispered.

"Yes," Magdalena replied. "We shall think of something."

----- X -----

In Finchley, The Hands was awoken from a dream of death and pain. Her eyes opened to find herself cramped in a bathtub with a shower head spraying her with cold water.

A voice in her head commanded, "Get up."

Maxine Elsworth could barely move. Her hands shuddered and her legs were in a terrible cramp. "I can't move," she stammered. "Where am I?"

"You died," the voice said. "But I need your help and I shall grant you extended life that you may fulfil your servitude to me."

Suddenly the realisation hit. "My LORD!" she cried out. "Command me." With effort, she found the edge of the bathtub and raised herself over the lip, collapsing to the bathroom floor. Her arms and legs fought against the first signs of rigor mortis, her mind struggled to clear away the fog from an oxygen starved brain. "What is your bidding, my Lord."

"Stand," the voice replied.

Maxine fought with gritted teeth to pull upright and as she did took sight of herself in the mirror. All of the hair from the front of her head was burned away, her exposed breasts and face had peeled back to blackened muscle, her eyes were glowing white orbs against the grizzled carnage. "I am ready, my Lord, for your instruction."

"I know you are," said the voice. "I know you are. And I have very special work for you. Serve me well, and your rewards will be amongst the greatest I have ever offered."

"What shall I do first, my Lord."

The voice spoke deeper, a growl of almost animal character. "Be my lieutenant on Earth. Be my earthly presence."

"I shall, my Lord. With the greatest honour, I shall."

EPILOGUE

The lights of the morgue clicked on. The fluorescent strips bathed the room in a powerful white light. The coroner led the Chief Inspector and his associate to a wall of steel drawers. He opened the door slightly then looked at his visitors to ensure they were ready. The Inspector wore the full uniform with epaulets and a cap, the man with him was somewhat academic; bald on top with tufts of white hair at the sides and a bowtie, he had the air of an eccentric university professor.

"The body started changing almost as soon as it was brought in." The coroner opened the door fully and slid out the steel tray holding the decapitated remains of the woman. Her leathery black skin was cracking and showing raised edges of what looked like writing. Her whole body was covered in an articulate script. "I don't know what to make of it," the coroner said. "I've not seen anything like it before. That writing wasn't there when she came in."

The professorly man got closer and began examining a portion of script in detail. He read it aloud as an indecipherable mumble that may have been another language.

"We know this woman," the Inspector said. "She

233

had a lot of tattoos which is what you're seeing now."

"No," the coroner said, "I know what a tattoo looks like. Those markings have just started to develop."

"They're just tattoos," the Inspector said a little more forcefully. "And I'm going to insist on a full criminal autopsy to be carried out under Met supervision, so please don't make any further progress with this body until authorised to do so."

----- X -----

In Covent Garden, Herbert Raphael smoothed back the tufts of white hair by his temples and entered the Masonic Temple through the rear loading bay; or rather, he entered the smaller doorway beside it. He followed the stairs down to a fire door with the legend DO NOT BLOCK stencilled across it. Beyond that door he used a key to open a store room door and once inside used another key to make his way into the Temple of Other.

The walls were decorated with a fine port-coloured wallpaper and the seats upholstered in chocolate leather. It looked like the lounge of a traditional gentleman's club save for the giant circular vault door at the rear. The main door was already open but the interior had a steel cage as a final barrier. There were no bars of gold to be seen on the shelves, but books and objects. Leather bound tomes and crystal balls, brass devices of intricate but unknown purpose. A vintage brass microscope stood on one shelf beside a small wooden box inlaid with silver elephants. A mummified hand was under glass. A malformed human head in a jar of preservative fluid.

Herbert Raphael made his way into the vault and found two men in dark suits. "Mister Raphael," one of them said. "Is it true you have found an Eye?"

Herbert took a roll of white cotton from inside his suit jacket and carefully unrolled it to show the dagger at the centre. "It is, Mister Carson. I present you the Eye of Magdalena."

Both men drew close but it was Carson who lifted it. "My God, it is a wonder."

"There is something else, Sir. I visited the cavern below the Almassy Legal Partnership and there's no question it was a cult. That's where the Eye was found. Outside the building, a woman was killed by decapitation and her body has begun to show words and scripts. It is written in the language of the One True Lord."

Carson carefully carried the Eye of Magdalena to the deepest end of the vault. "And what does it say?"

"Secrets, Sir."

Carson lifted the Eye of Magdalena to meet its two siblings. On a shelf, under a small pin spot of light was the Eye of Jacob and the Eye of Elijah. "Secrets, you say?" He fixed his eyes on the three knives and took a step back to admire them. Three knives with whalebone handles, all crafted with ornate designs, each with a ruby gemstone in the hilt. "The real secret is why the Eyes are coming together?"

"Indeed it is, Sir." Herbert Raphael replied.

"So, what secrets are revealed on this corpse?"
"All of them, Mister Carson. All of them."

In memory of Jonathan McGeorge
1977-2017

Books by Lee McGeorge

Gingerbread Economy
Vampire "Untitled"
Vampire "Unseen"
Vampire "Unleashed"
Clair Noto's The Tourist
Slenderman, Slenderman, Take this Child
The Thing: Zero Day
Videodrome: Days of O'Blivion
Mister Deathmask
The Obsidian

You can chat with the author on Facebook.
http://www.facebook.com/leemcgeorge73

29123971R00139

Printed in Great Britain
by Amazon